CHAPTER 1
A REASON TO DIE

Devante knew he couldn't tell her the truth when his mother asked, "Are you sure you're going to be okay?"

This was it. They had finally arrived at his school. They were parked in front of the main entrance, just like so many times before, just like nothing had changed. Sleepy-looking teenagers streamed in from every direction. They were getting out of their parents' cars or crossing the overpass and coming from the 'L' train station, bright kids drawn from all corners of Chicago to this magnet school conveniently located near a major expressway. Some carried backpacks weighed down with complicated textbooks, some carried lunches, some struggled with cumbersome science or art projects, others lugged musical instruments. Some wore headphones so they could listen to music, others were talking to the friends they walked with. A few wore ROTC uniforms. Some others even wore business suits.

Who are they again? Future Business Executives of America or something? He tried to remember. His school had lots of clubs like that for future leaders, future soldiers, future doctors, future lawyers...

Devante no longer believed in the future.

Across the street from the high school, the cadets at the police academy—future cops—were lining up in the parking lot, preparing for their morning run. For all of them, these hopeful students looking to the future, it was just another day at school. Just another Friday morning. It was amazing that the lives of those around him continued to go on, while for Devante time seemed to stand still.

"Look at me," his mother urged him.

She was insistent, but she didn't sound angry. Just worried. In the past few weeks, it had become hard for him to make eye contact with anyone, even his own reflection.

"Look at me," she said again as she cupped his chin in her hand and turned his face toward her.

His eyelids seemed to weigh a ton. It was as if all the tears he refused to cry had collected in them. Still, he couldn't let his mother know how much the events of the past month had affected him.

"I'm fine, Ma. Really. I am." He grabbed his bag quickly and hoped he could get out of the door before his mother realized that everything he had just said was a lie. He flung the heavy door open and rushed out of the car so fast, the cold March air scarcely had time to come in. He slammed the door shut and was startled by the sound.

With slow, measured steps he approached his school, the place he'd been trying to avoid for the past three weeks. He turned around and saw his mother pulling away. She had driven him here herself this morning because she wanted to make sure he went back. And he had gone because he thought he would be able to pretend he was okay.

I can do this, he thought as he reached the entrance. Swarms of kids were beginning to fill the halls. He could see them through the large front windows. Hopefully they wouldn't notice him. Maybe they would avoid him, just as they had after the funeral. So far he was in luck. He didn't see any familiar faces...until he noticed a big poster on an easel outside the principal's office.

It was a portrait of Monica.

It was the photo they showed on the news and in the papers, the one they had used in the programs at the funeral home. Her eyes and smile were forever frozen, looking out at him in tragic stillness. And now he was also still, standing by the front door, realizing that the numbness he'd felt the past few weeks was wearing off.

He was wrong. He couldn't go in.

He saw a couple walk by, holding hands as if they were the last two people left on earth, or the last ones left at Whitney Park High School. They were the kind of couple that would have showed up at homecoming in matching rayon shirts from Merry-Go-Round. Their smiles mocked his misery. He and Monica had been like them once, sauntering through the halls, sharing headphones, cocooned in a private world of music. Seeing that couple was a harsh reminder that he could never return to that world. He stayed on the outside, looking in, alone, and realized he was no longer like the other students.

How could he pretend he was still one of them? How could he smile or laugh when nothing seemed funny anymore? How could he act like anything still mattered? How could he and his parents meet with the school counselors this afternoon? What good would it do now that everything had permanently changed? He didn't have a reason to go to his classes. He didn't have a reason to study. He didn't have a reason to graduate. All he had was a reason to die.

He stood frozen for a moment, as though the frigid air that crept through his baggy jeans had stiffened his legs completely. Then he slowly backed away, turned around, and ran in the opposite direction.

Just go, he told himself, rushing forward on the sidewalk. *Don't look back. Don't even say goodbye.*

The wintry world around him seemed like it was already dead: gray sky, brown grass, skeletal trees. He stopped at the curb, right across the street from the overpass that bridged the expressway. If he jumped over the side of the overpass, would he die? If he fell, would anyone notice? If he died, would everything stop? Not waiting for the traffic lights to change, he ran across the street and skidded to a stop on the other side.

Now the overpass stretched out in front of him. Before, he had only seen it as a way to get to Burger King during fifth period lunch, but now it had taken on a new meaning. It was the bridge between life and death. The only thing that stopped him was the chain-link fence above the guardrails. He hurled his heavy book bag to the ground and began to climb.

I just want everything to stop. I just want all of it to be over, he thought. *To die. To sleep no more.* He vaguely remembered the words from a play he had read last semester in freshman English. He wondered if Hamlet had nightmares too.

As he stood on the guardrail, a part of him hesitated. Part of him wanted someone to notice him up there. Part of him wanted someone to show him that he still had a reason to live. But he had to ignore those parts of himself now.

The weight of the metal ankh pendant around his neck, the ancient Egyptian symbol of life, felt ironic. The metal links of the fence were cold in his hands. He looked down at the traffic below, wondering which would kill him: the fall or a car. Whichever it was, he hoped it would be quick. What good hoping, though? It wouldn't bring Monica back. There was nothing he could do to make things right. The only thing he could do was jump.

"Hey kid!"

He turned to see a man and a woman from the police academy running toward him from across the street.

They're just toy cops anyway. They can't do anything. He turned back to face the expressway.

"Get down from there!" one of the toy cops yelled.

What're you gonna do? Arrest me for taking my life? Was that just one of the lessons they taught toy cops, how to arrest a Black guy for no reason? Why weren't they ever around when they could be useful?

They were on his side of the street now, but he still wouldn't move. He held on to the chain-link fence and stared down at the sluggish river of morning rush hour traffic below. He couldn't go back to school. He couldn't go back home. He had nowhere to go but down.

"We want to help you," one of them said.

"Leave me alone!"

They were breaking his concentration. How could he jump with them watching?

"Come on, kid. You're too young to throw your life away."

What does he know about my life?

"Just leave me here and let me die!"

But the toy cops rescued him in spite of himself.

He hadn't asked to be saved. He didn't want this. Once again he found himself somewhere between life and death. There were no words for what he felt.

When the real cops got involved, they asked him for his name. He showed them his school ID card. He had no reason to speak. He refused to say his parents' names. Instead, he wrote them down on a sheet of paper, along with their pager numbers. It wasn't long before he was rushed from the squad room where he'd sat with a policewoman who wouldn't let him out of her sight to the emergency room of the closest hospital.

There were a lot of hospitals in this part of town, just across the expressway from his school. The doctor who had come in to talk to his health class was from this hospital, and had told them they were welcome to stop by any time for free condoms. But the place where he was taken was not nearly as welcoming as the doctor had promised. There were bars on the windows and every door locked behind him. And by the time his parents finally got there, he had locked his voice away as well.

CHAPTER 2
QUIET STORM

This is my very own book and I'm gonna write anything I want to in here, just like I did in my other journals. All the crazy thoughts that run through my mind will fall into place on these pages. That's right, I'm crazy and I know it, so nobody has to tell me that. And I kinda like living in this mental institution, even though Dr. Lutkin hates it when I call it that. But that's what it is.

Sure, we go on field trips, and I have to go to classes every day, but then there's all the therapy I have after class and on weekends. I mean, there's group therapy, drug therapy, drama therapy, pet therapy, recreational therapy, occupational therapy, dance therapy, and music therapy. But my favorite is still art therapy.

Even writing in this journal is therapy. That's why

my parents give me a new one for my birthday every year. But Dr. Lutkin says that I've reached a plateau. He says I need to interact more with the other kids. And I would, except other than being crazy, we really don't have that much in common. Alejandra hates me most of the time, especially when she's manic. They switched her to a different psychiatrist last year and she blames me for it. She says I stole Dr. Lutkin from her. Ed avoids me because he thinks my thrift store clothes may have once belonged to dead people. I do talk to Marcia, though I'm not sure how much she understands since she believes The Brady Bunch is her real family. Joey and Kathleen don't talk much to anyone.

All of them have been here the longest. Then there are the kids who don't have to stay that long, the sojourners. It's cool to meet new people, but then they're gone as soon as you get to know them.

It would be nice to have a good friend. Or a boyfriend. I'm not sure when I'll get to go home, but honestly, I'm kinda scared to leave. People out there don't like me. But things weren't so bad at the thrift store the other day. Meredith took some of us there on a field trip. Marcia just has to have her 70s clothes. She can't live in

1994 with the rest of us. While I was there, I found a really fly red kimono. It's short, but it has long, long sleeves that will just get in the way, so I'm gonna trim them the next time we can do some sewing with Libby in occupational therapy. I want to wear it with jeans. After we left the thrift store, I got some boots at the army surplus store. They're not Doc Martens, but I really like them. The people at the thrift store and the army surplus store were all really nice to us. They treated us like normal customers. Then again, everyone else shopping there had rainbow-colored hair and piercings in their faces, so maybe we looked pretty normal compared to them.

Keep a secret for me: While we were on our way back, Zack told me the shadows under the 'L' tracks reveal a secret message in a special code only he can understand. He made me promise not to tell anyone else about it. Weird, right? Just another day in the life of a crazy girl.

Anyway, besides this journal, I got two other birthday presents from my parents: a new Cross Colours outfit and a dress that's beautiful beyond the speed of light. Of course it's still too cold to wear it yet. I can't wait for it to warm up so I can finally put it on. Maybe with my new combat boots. I'm so happy I don't have to wear a uniform anymore like I did before I came here. Who would have thought that a mental hospital-excuse me, a special school for crazy kids-would be less strict than a regular private school? I actually feel more free in here than I ever did out there.

Janina stopped writing in her journal and closed it so she could admire its cover. It was decorated with a smiling yellow sun and bright daisies. It was the kind of retro thing Marcia would love. The bright colors, she knew, were a kind of therapy in themselves. They were supposed to brighten her mood and lift her out of her depression. That was the basic idea the school was designed around, it seemed. And sometimes that worked for her. Other times, it seemed like all that brightness just created deeper shadows. Because despite all the cheerful colors, the sadness of her fellow students felt almost contagious at times.

She could hear the winter wind wail and moan as it whipped around her little corner room. It reminded her of someone crying, like Alejandra when she got really depressed. But now, except for the wind, things were quiet. It was probably almost time for bed, but maybe there was enough time to work on her graphic novel.

She got her sketchbook from the top of the pile of books beside her bed. She was always reading something. There were so many different subjects she was interested in, and Dr. Lutkin sometimes loaned her psychology books he said would help her understand herself better. Reading helped her understand the other kids better, too. When she was eleven, she saw her classmate Courtney have a seizure after taking her medication. After that, Janina refused to take her pills for fear that it might happen to her. Though everyone told her that she had nothing to worry about because what she'd seen was caused by Courtney's medical condition, Janina wasn't convinced until her teacher had her write a report on epilepsy. And that had led to her learning about the nervous system and the parts of the brain.

Still, she often imagined what it would be like if the pills they took had strange side effects. Or what if the medication made them turn into mutants like the X-Men or the Ninja Turtles, and gave them superpowers? What if it was all part of some weird experiment? Eventually she started writing down her ideas and drawing pictures of her characters. Combining her love of words and pictures led to her graphic novel. Her main character was Steffanie, a brave and beautiful girl whose depression medication made her have seizures. But she discovered that when she had seizures, she had out-of-body experiences and could go anywhere she wanted to. The other kids in the mental hospital with her also had psychic powers because of their medication. And because they had different illnesses, they had different powers. At first Janina was going to call her story "Crazy Pill

Syndrome", but after reading a book about people with psychic powers, she changed the title to "Psindrome".

The "psi" was for the special psychic powers the kids had in her story. She grabbed a pen and started drawing and writing about Steffanie's latest predicament.

Why am I here? Why are they rolling me into this elevator? Why am I in the basement now? Where are they taking me? Who are they? Steffanie asked herself these questions through every step of her strange journey. And with each question, she felt more and more awake. Her mounting fear and uncertainty would not allow her weary eyes to close.

At last they reached a familiar corridor. The masked doctors took her into a room across the hall from the lab where Sparky used to live.

"You can get up now."

"What are you going to do to me?" Steffanie demanded.

One of the doctors approached her. "Don't worry, Steffanie. We're not going to hurt you. We're just going to do a few tests."

"What kinds of tests?"

"It's really quite simple. We're going to study your brain."

That was when Steffanie remembered the dream

she had once told Dr. Weaver about. Was he trying to make it real?

"No! I won't let you!"

Janina wondered what she should write next. Sometimes in her room, when no one was looking, she would use the Barbies and Kens she still had to act out scenes from her story. It was like making a miniature movie. She kept them in a plastic Caboodles box under her bed. The Skipper doll playing the part of Steffanie laid in a bed in Janina's hospital play set.

She held a Ken doll in a white coat menacingly over Steffanie. "All we're going to do is use the equipment we have. We'll study your brain waves and later we'll use the MRI machine to scan images of your brain."

She picked up her pen to sketch the scene she'd just set up. And then there was a soft knock at the door. She saw Meredith, one of the counselors, peeking in through the window at the top.

"Lights out," Meredith stuck her head in the door and said.

"Okay." Janina sighed, putting down her sketchbook and pen.

As usual she had lost track of time while she was working on her story. She wished she could stay up a little bit later, but she had to follow the rules.

"Good night." Meredith smiled before turning out the light and closing the door.

Janina would have to figure out Steffanie's daring escape from the evil psychiatrists tomorrow. It might even come to her in a dream. It was a good thing she had at least remembered to change into her pajamas before she started writing in her new journal. Maybe she wasn't a complete space cadet after all. All she had to do now was wrap her hair for the night in the colorful silk scarf her mother gave her. She took her two long braids and wound them around her head, folded the big square scarf into a triangle, and tied it up. She wanted to make it look like one of the headwraps the African women in one of her favorite old picture books wore, but she could never get it just right, and could never get the scarf to stay on her head while she slept.

She picked up her Snuggle bear. He was just as soft and cuddly as the one that came to life on the fabric softener commercials, though worn from years of squeezing. When she found out she'd be going to the Harrison School when she was ten years old, Snuggle was the first thing she packed in her suitcase. She'd moved to her single room from the one she had shared with three other girls when she was twelve, and Snuggle had been sitting in front of her pillow all this time.

She took him into her arms and held him, but imagined what it would be like if he were a boy and not a teddy bear. She closed her eyes and kissed his mouth. Then she reached inside an undone seam in Snuggle's stitching and pulled out her headphones. She wasn't supposed to have headphones. She had bought a cheap pair at Woolworth's when the counselors who'd brought them there on a field trip weren't looking. Dr. Lutkin didn't allow headphones because he said they were too isolating, and had explained to her the difference between privacy and isolation. But that was one rule she didn't see the point of following. She plugged her headphones into the radio on the nightstand beside her bed. She had it tuned to her favorite R&B station, something her parents wouldn't like since their church didn't want its members listening to anything but Gospel music. The station was playing slow jams now.

"Up next on Quiet Storm, it's 'Alone With You' by Tevin Campbell," crooned an announcer with a deep voice as smooth as velvet. Janina let the music envelop her and drifted off to sleep.

CHAPTER 3
BETTER THAN NOTHING

Dear Shawn,

It's always been hard for me to picture Dr. Hoffman actually working as a psychiatrist. As an auditor for the IRS, sure. Or as a bill collector, or a drill sergeant, or even as a standup comedienne who specializes in insult humor. When she was my professor, she always had a sneaky way of getting into our heads and making us question the things we thought we knew. A lot of times she would answer our questions with questions of her own. She put me through a lot when she taught me. I thought when I graduated from med school I had seen the last of her, but I was so wrong. Guess who got promoted? Guess who is now in charge of supervising all the future psychiatrists at the university's inpatient child and adolescent ward?

That's right, little brother: Dr. Hoffman, the one and only.

I can picture her marching through the corridors, a flock of white-coated interns trailing her like little ducklings who know no better than to follow the first leader they see. (That's called imprinting, by the way.) Now, as if things aren't bad enough, Dr. Hoffman was the one I had to talk to today. My worst professor is now my only hope.

Her first question: "What was your reason for leaving your residency at Haven House?"

If Dr. Hoffman had seen Haven House, she'd understand. So I tried to paint a picture for her. I told her it's a miserable place full of cold white walls and miserable kids. It's clinical and unadorned, like an operating room. No, not unadorned; deliberately stripped of anything resembling character, making it a place that was no place at all. Sure, it has a nice lobby to impress the parents when they come to visit, but the rest of it looks like the kind of mental institution you see in movies. When I worked there, I realized for the first time just how different the standard of care was for kids whose illnesses were mental and not physical. If children with cancer or AIDS had been treated as my patients had, you would hear about it on the news. But to the staff at Haven House, and maybe to the rest of the world, the patients were nothing but problem children.

I even told Dr. Hoffman about the first time I saw the patients getting what the chief resident called "chair therapy." In a long corridor, kids sat in their chairs, facing the wall. They weren't allowed to speak to each other or the staff, or even give anyone eye contact. More than anything I wanted to reach out to them, to be there for them, to listen to what they had to say. I thought that was what I was supposed to do. When I worked in the other hospital last year, the one for adults, that was what I had done. But when I tried that at Haven House, I got in trouble. Just as they weren't allowed to speak to me, I wasn't allowed to speak to them!

Shawn, when I say these were kids, I don't mean they were all teenagers like you. One boy looked like he was only ten years old, and he was crying. Anywhere else, any other doctor would go talk to him to make sure he was okay. I think of all the times you were scared going to the dentist or getting a shot at the doctor's office.

They never just left you there crying. But things are different at Haven House. At Haven House, silently facing a wall for hours on end is just part of the "behavior modification program."

It was frightening to think this was how they did things there, at one of the most expensive mental hospitals for kids in the northern suburbs. I wondered if the parents who sent their children there had any idea. It wasn't a place where sick kids could get better. It was a place where rich kids were basically held hostage. If that place was supposed to be one of the best, what did that mean for the specialty I had chosen?

Of course somehow, the patients were always miraculously "cured" the day their insurance ran out. It didn't matter if the kids were better - just that their bills were being paid. The worst was a boy being sent home too soon. He was still depressed - anyone could see that. I was worried about him. His first day out, he deliberately crashed his car into a tree and shattered both his legs. He'll probably need several operations before he can walk again, if he can ever walk at all. Nobody at Haven House even seemed to care except for me. That was when I knew I had to leave.

After I told Dr. Hoffman all of this, she asked me if Haven House was a for-profit hospital. I told her yes, and that they're owned by PHEA. Dr. Hoffman wasn't surprised. PHEA has gotten in a lot of trouble lately, though many of the other companies that ran mental hospitals and were in it for the money got in so much trouble that they had to go to a big hearing in Washington before Congress about a year ago. Most of those companies are going out of business now. I could tell by the look on Dr. Hoffman's face that she hates PHEA just as much as I do. I felt relieved that we had an enemy in common. I hoped it meant she would understand why I quit my residency so suddenly.

I also explained to her that Haven House hadn't been my first choice. I told her I'd wanted to work at the hospital she's in charge of now, but I didn't get matched. Then she told me she was the one who rejected me from the program!

She said, "Frankly, I found your credentials lacking. You didn't major in psychology as an undergraduate, you took a leave of absence after your first year of medical school, and you changed specialties shortly after you returned.

And you really struggled in my class. There were too many red flags. I had to reject you."

I was stunned. All this time I thought I had been randomly matched to Haven House by a computer, not turned down for the program I wanted to work for by an old teacher who didn't like me. But knowing that, I couldn't let Dr. Hoffman's opinions about me keep me from getting a good opportunity.

So I did my best to explain myself. I told her I knew what she meant about red flags because I saw them at Haven House from the first day I worked there, but decided not to pay any attention to them. Even though I knew things weren't right, I tried my best to make it work. I ignored my own instincts until I couldn't ignore them anymore. I told her that even though I didn't major in psychology in college, I learned a lot about human nature from all the stories and poems I read as an English major. I explained that now, to make up for all the things I didn't learn in college, I'm reading as many psychology books as I can.

I didn't go into all the details of my leave of absence. You know why I couldn't. I just told her that something happened to someone I cared about and it made me see the value of psychiatry. What I've learned hasn't come from taking all the right classes at all the right times. It's come from having my life turned upside down.

Then I asked her who a troubled kid can relate to more, someone who has always had it easy, or someone who knows how tough life can be and didn't have to read about it in a textbook? After all, isn't that what our profession is all about, helping people cope with what life throws at them?

I tried to sound confident even though I was so nervous and so scared that she would tell me no. I think I was trying to convince myself as much as Dr. Hoffman that I really wanted to job. Because honestly—and I know I've never told you this—I started having my doubts about psychiatry from my very first day at Haven House. I've always been worried I'm not good enough and might end up making a terrible mistake. Sometimes I still wonder if I should have made the switch from radiology. It's so much easier to look at the pictures we can take with MRI machines or x-rays and understand what's wrong with people. I like feeling certain. But I told you why I switched. I promised you I would see it through.

I want to be a good sister and keep my promise.

I think I got through to Dr. Hoffman. After I stated my case, she said she needs to know she can rely on me and trust me to finish what I've started. She's not hiring any new residents until July, but wants me to prove I'm serious. She has an old friend who helped start a small boarding school for kids with emotional problems. She said she would call him to see if he would hire me as one of his counselors, and that if things go well, she'll consider me.

The whole thing makes me uneasy. What if there are no openings for counselors? What if Dr. Hoffman's friend is just as hard to please as she is? What if things don't work out at the school? What can I do, go back home to California? You know I still can't. There are too many ghosts there, too many wrongs that can never be righted.

So Dr. Hoffman's offer is better than nothing. She promised to call as soon as she hears from her old friend. So much depends on that phone call. What if I've come to the end of my career before it even begins? After all I went through to apply to medical school and then finish, could all of my time have been wasted? I have worked so hard and wanted so much, and now here

I am so close to finishing what I started, yet so close to losing it all. I don't deal well with such uncertainty.

On my way out of Dr. Hoffman's office, I saw someone I knew from medical school. I told you about Omar before. He's seventeen now, and is about to start his internship. I don't know him very well, but I always make sure I speak to him so he won't feel out of place. It must be tough being a teenager in medical school. Omar wants to be a brain surgeon, so he really has his work cut out for him. But at least he knows what he wants to do.

"You'll probably be board-certified before I am," I joked.

When Omar smiled at me, I suddenly knew that I still want to work with teenagers more than anything else.

For now, I wait. I already had a chance to get things organized around here and be a better roommate to Anjali. I even figured out what to do with some of my old things from med school. Beetlejuice the model skeleton is wearing my white coat.

If wanting to put my medical training to use wasn't a good enough reason to make me want to go out into the world and do something useful, daytime television certainly is. With Anjali out delivering babies, the TV has been my only companion since I quit my residency. You know I always liked talk shows better than soap operas, but there are only so many times I can watch people on Oprah, Jenny Jones, Ricki Lake, and Sally Jessy Raphael make their private lives public. Then there are the ads for The Psychic Friends Network, vague commercials for a new antidepressant ("Denoxamine - ask your doctor"), and the worst offender: "If you don't get help for your troubled teen at Haven House, please get help somewhere." Reruns of 'Quincy' are all that have sustained me. Watching him go on a crusade to find the truth behind the medical mysteries he solves reminds me of why I wanted to become a doctor in the first place. Hopefully soon the phone will ring and I will have another chance to prove myself.

Devante sat uneasily in the waiting area. It seemed wrong to him that he should be uncomfortable in such a nice chair, in a lobby with marble floors and a chandelier overhead, but he was. This place really was a school, much to his surprise. It looked a lot like some of the fancy private prep schools his father had taken him to visit, where he was almost always the only Black kid taking the tour. He hadn't known what to expect when he walked in with his family and overheard his father ask his mother if his school had sent his test scores. He wasn't sure what would happen next. This place was a welcome sight after spending the last seventy-two hours locked in a cage, too tense to eat or sleep. It seemed like a nice place, maybe nicer than he deserved.

He could hear his parents shouting from inside the doctor's office. It had been almost a year since he'd heard them fighting, their voices muffled behind closed doors. Hearing it again made him feel a shiver of self-blame. He knew they were fighting about him. His parents' arguments were epic battles, the collision of an immovable force and an irresistible object, a war of words between two angry lawyers without a judge to mediate. Two lawyers who had, on separate occasions, given him two very different definitions of what the phrase "irreconcilable differences" meant.

He could imagine what they were probably saying.

Dad: "You should never have brought him to that neighborhood with all those ghetto lowlife welfare queens and their gangbanger kids!"

Mom: "I only wanted him to know about his heritage and where he came from. My family had to fight to buy that house. And it's a working class neighborhood. Don't you dare call it a ghetto!"

"That's not the kind of environment I want my son to live in."

"Devante is my son, too!"

"I named him Herbert! What kind of ridiculous name is Devante? Why did you give him that low-class middle name? Why does he insist on being called by that name, so he can fit in with the rest of the neighborhood hoodlums? And that ghetto girl he was friends with—"

He thought of the overpass.

Shoulda ignored those toy cops. Shoulda jumped.

He heard footsteps in the hall. It was Dr.

Lutkin, the psychiatrist who had given him some tests to take while his parents toured the school. The tests were multiple choice, though the questions were like nothing he'd ever seen.

In the past 6 months, have you experienced the following:

Your parents' divorce

Moving to a new house

Starting at a new school

Being the victim of a violent crime

The death of a close friend or relative

His answer to all of them was "yes."

Dr. Lutkin looked at him before heading into his office. He didn't say anything, which was probably smart since Devante wouldn't have replied. There was something reassuring about that brief glance. When their eyes met, Devante felt understood. A White man with gray hair and full beard, Dr. Lutkin looked the way Devante expected a psychiatrist to look, but with cooler eyeglasses. The volume of his parents' voices got louder when Dr. Lutkin opened the door, then quieted after it shut.

Everything felt so hollow to him, and so unreal. He had wanted everything to stop, but instead he kept living and it all just kept going. His mind had become like a factory that only manufactured two things: panic and sadness. And that was why he'd wanted to shut down his mind's machinery. What would falling have felt like? What would he have felt like just before he hit the ground? Would he have finally felt free?

Dr. Lutkin opened the door again and Devante's parents walked out. Both of them looked upset and confused.

Was what the doctor said about me really that bad?   "Devante, I'd like to speak to you for a fe minutes," Dr. Lutkin said.

Devante got up and went into the office. Dr. Lutkin shut the door behind them. Good. His parents wouldn't be able to listen in. Or maybe it wasn't good. Maybe it would be easier if they were here in the room with him. He took a seat in front of Dr. Lutkin's desk, feeling uncomfortable in another comfortable chair. He was sure that now the doctor was going to tell him he was hopelessly insane before throwing him into a dungeon or a padded cell. Not that it mattered. He was pretty sure nothing worse could happen now. What could be worse than already being dead inside?

Much to his surprise, Dr. Lutkin said, "Whether you stay here or don't, it's your decision."

His decision? He didn't know he had a choice. On Friday, they had just taken him to that hospital and locked him up.

"If you stay, we can help you get well. You don't have to keep feeling the way you've been feeling the past few weeks. But I'm not going to force you to stay. This has to be your choice. Do you want to stay?"

Devante studied Dr. Lutkin's face. He seemed to be telling the truth. Devante wasn't being forced. He was being asked. He was being invited. And they could help him here. He still didn't say anything. There were no words. His pain was so unspeakable.

Then Dr. Lutkin got up from his desk.

"Since you didn't respond, I guess that means you want to go."

Dr. Lutkin walked over to the door and opened it. Devante could see his parents sitting in the lobby. He couldn't go back home now—wherever home was anymore—and live with either of them. This place might be safe. He wanted to stay. But he couldn't open his mouth to say it. Instead, he got up and closed the door. Then he sat back down in the chair, which felt more comfortable now, and looked at Dr. Lutkin.

"I see you want to stay," Dr. Lutkin said with a smile. "Welcome."

Dr. Lutkin opened the door again, and Devante's parents came into the room. Now they looked relieved. His mom gave him a hug. His father gave him his overnight bag. Dr. Lutkin gave him a diagnosis: something called Acute Stress Disorder.

"Before you go to your new room, you and your parents need to understand that you won't be in contact with each other until the end of the week. After that, you can have regular visits. Nurse Erica will see you to your room."

The nurse introduced herself and walked with him down a hallway that had bright murals painted on its walls, then up a flight of stairs that were each painted a different color. They turned a corner and went up another set of stairs to the third floor. Somehow as he studied his new surroundings, he overlooked the girl who stood timidly near the top of the stairs, smiling at him. The staircase led to a wide room with big arched windows and lime green walls. There were couches, a TV, a ping pong table, and the biggest beanbag chairs he'd ever seen. This was the lounge, the nurse explained. It connected two wings of the building.

"Your room is in the boys' wing, through these doors. You're not allowed to visit the girls' wing without permission and supervision from a counselor."

Devante nodded. His head felt heavier now, as did his eyelids. The nurse unlocked the door and showed him into his new room. It was small, just the right size for one person. The walls were blue, and the doors and drawers on the wood furniture were all painted different colors. Instead of being made up, the covers on the bed were folded back, ready for him to sleep there. The sheets were dark blue and inviting. He sat down on the foot of the bed and dropped his bag at his feet, then took off his shoes.

"You can keep your shoes, but I need to take the laces," Nurse Erica explained.

But by now he felt so exhausted that unlacing his shoes seemed too complicated a task. So he gave them to the nurse and got in bed, still in his jeans. Changing into his pajamas was too much work.

"Do you need anything to help you stay asleep? I can get something if you'd like."

He shook his head. There was no need. The exhaustion of the past few weeks of sleepless nights had finally caught up to him. He was asleep as soon as his head hit the pillow.

"So how did you celebrate your birthday?" Dr. Lutkin asked Janina. She hadn't seen him since last week, before her parents had come by for a Friday night celebration.

"Did you go home?"

Home. She flinched at the word.

"Not this time," she replied. "My parents came and brought me some presents and cake, and a new journal. It was nice."

Dr. Lutkin seemed disappointed. "Another birthday at this place?"

He'd said it like it was a bad thing, but she liked it here. She liked her room. She liked his office. When she was younger, it was because had the best toys out of all the therapists at Harrison. There were dolls, action figures, a castle with a working drawbridge, toy cars, trucks, trains, planes, stuffed animals, and an amazing three-story dollhouse. It had two staircases and working electric lights. Playing with it had been part of her therapy. They didn't do play therapy any more, but she still liked to look at the dollhouse during her sessions. Sometimes she still imagined being five inches tall and living inside of it and growing tiny flowers in the window boxes. It helped her relax.

Now that she was older, she had come to admire what she thought of as Dr. Lutkin's library, the wall of bookshelves behind his desk on the other side of his office. He had so many books about so many different things. She hoped to have a big collection like that of her own someday. And she liked his furniture, especially the cool purple chairs that looked retro and futuristic at the same time, where they sat during her sessions.

"I don't mind. I'd rather be here. I don't really like it out there."

Actually, that was an understatement. Other than going on field trips with the other kids, Janina never left the school, especially not to go home with her parents. When they wanted to see her, they had to visit. She refused to go anywhere with them. And that was why they came to see her on the weekends, usually on Friday nights. Her mother, who was a beautician, even styled Janina's hair for her, right there in her room. But lately Dr. Lutkin had been talking to Janina a lot about going home, a topic she hated discussing.

"You can't let a few bad experiences get you down." He'd told her the same thing many times before. The bad experiences he spoke of had mainly happened when she was allowed to go home with her family during the summers. She would never forget how mean those girls had been to her, and all because they knew about where she went to school now. They used to be her classmates.

"Whenever anybody's about to get in trouble," one of them said, "all the teachers have to say is, 'Remember what happened to Janina? Do you want to get sent away to the nuthouse, too?'"

All of them laughed at her. What made it worse was that they were her neighbors. So pretty soon, even the kids who went to public school knew about it, too. Janina couldn't go outside without them teasing her. Finally, when she was twelve, a new girl about her age moved in next door and she thought she had a new friend...

She didn't want to think about that now. She could still feel the sting of all those rejections. She told her parents she thought she had agoraphobia and didn't want to leave the house, so they let her go back to Harrison a week earlier than they'd planned. And that had been the last time she'd gone home. Everyone kept saying she needed to get over it, especially Dr. Lutkin.

"I know," she told him sadly.

She wished she could be like the girls she read about in *Seventeen* or saw on TV shows about teenagers. Again she wondered if she would ever fit in with normal people or become normal herself. Wasn't it easier to just hide from everyone?

Here I go again.

She was supposed to be working on being more positive. She tried to find something positive to think about. There was one thing that had happened today that made her smile: She'd seen a new boy in the hallway earlier. He was tall and wore his hair in a high top fade that made him look even taller, and he wore baggy jeans and an oversized vest with big pockets and a Cross Colours hoodie, and he was so handsome he reminded her of some of the singers she liked. It had been a bittersweet encounter, as he hadn't even noticed her, let alone the shy smile she gave him.

Should I even tell Dr. Lutkin about that? Well, he did say I could talk to him about anything.

"The new boy is really cute," she said. "I saw him when I was on my way to class. I wish I could ask you about him, but I know you can't really tell me anything."

"Sorry, but you're right. I can't."

"Yeah, that wouldn't be fair." Surely whatever the new boy told Dr. Lutkin was just as confidential as what Janina told him. But eventually she'd find out in group therapy or something.

"But maybe you could talk to him yourself." Dr. Lutkin surprised her.

"Me?"

"Sure, why not? I've got an idea. But first, you have to promise that if you do this, you won't say anything to him about dating. Don't even ask if he has a girlfriend."

How strange. She had just read an article in *Seventeen* called "How to Ask a Guy if He Already Has a Girlfriend". Under normal circumstances, shouldn't she try to find that out somehow? But she wasn't normal, and neither was he.

"Okay."

"Good. You gave me your word. So how about giving him a tour of the building tomorrow afternoon instead of going to your social skills group?"

It would be so nice not to have to go to social skills, a group that was comprised of her, Kathleen, Joey, and a rotating cast of uncommunicative people. The whole point of it was to practice having conversations with other people her own age. It was never quite as easy as that, though.

There was something sad and sweet about Kathleen, and Janina tried talking to her during the group exercises. When she did talk, much of what Kathleen said made sense only to her alone, though Janina did her best to follow her meandering stories about being visited by a series of red ripe tomatoes. The only thing Kathleen had told Janina that she understood was that she felt like she didn't belong anywhere. Hiding behind the cascade of rust colored coils and ringlets that got their color from her mother and their texture from her father, she seemed so uncomfortable in her light brown skin because she was neither Black nor White. When Janina tried to talk, though, Kathleen was often too distracted by voices that only she could hear to really listen.

Recently the group had gotten some new members: Raven, a goth girl who only talked about cemeteries, Kyle, who was always trying to finish everyone else's sentences, and Heather, who lied about everything. Giving the new boy a tour instead would be much better.

"Yeah, I can do that."

She could hardly believe it. She was going to get a chance to spend time with him. She was glad she'd spoken up.

"And another thing: If he doesn't talk to you, don't take it personally, okay?"

"Okay."

She tried to sound positive about it even though her heart sank at the thought of the boy's silence. It was hard enough having to deal with Kathleen and Joey. But maybe this boy was different.

Dr. Lutkin looked at his watch. She knew what that meant. Their time was up for the day. But before she left, he had a gift for her. He took a book from one of his many shelves and gave it to her. Its title was *Modern American Poetry*, but it hadn't been modern for a long time. It was yellowed with age, and the worn cover made Janina think this books must be well-loved. Somehow it seemed even more valuable to her than if it had been new. Both she and Dr. Lutkin really liked poetry. They talked about it sometimes in her sessions. It was so nice of him to remember that.

"Happy birthday." He smiled.

The restaurant in the atrium of the skyscraper was the kind that owed its existence to executive expense accounts. No one would come here for a birthday celebration, or a date, or a marriage proposal. It was built for business meetings. Tall palm trees stretched upward, pointing to the glass roof some 60 stories above them, an architectural crown that looked like the turret of a castle. A muscular sculpture of the Greek god Poseidon poured water that rushed loudly into a fountain surrounded by live plants. The yuppie businesspeople who sat at little tables spread across a wide expanse of cold white and gray marble all resembled one another. Dr. Lutkin felt out of place among them, the kind of people he called "squares" back when he was a teenager. Their suits were angular, their briefcases expensive-looking, their cell phones and laptops gray and bulky. One woman sat alone waiting. She was the picture of the successful 90s businesswoman, her hair and nails professionally styled, wearing a sharply tailored business suit that flattered her razor-thin frame.

Perhaps she was actually a little too thin, Dr. Lutkin thought once he got closer. Normally when he was away from the school, he shut off the part of his mind that diagnosed and analyzed and counseled. But over the years, noticing things like this had become a nervous habit, a way of quietly getting the upper hand over those who would try to overpower him, or keeping his mind occupied in tense or tedious situations. It was what he did to stay awake during boring meetings with executives from Psychiatric Hospital Enterprises of America. He thought again of the deal he had made with himself this morning: if he could just make it through this meeting, he would treat himself to a jazz concert at one of his favorite clubs afterwards. It was a little positive reinforcement to appease the restless teenage soul that still lived inside his middle-aged self. As he got closer to the table, he noticed the woman's skin had an unhealthy pallor. He came up to her table and shook her cold, bony hand.

"Rebecca, so good to finally meet you," he said, looking into her sunken eyes.

"Likewise. Sorry to have you come out in this weather. It's brutal out there! Haven't you people ever heard of spring?"

It did seem a little cruel, even for PHEA, to send her here from sunny Florida this time of year. Meteorologically speaking, though, it was still winter, too early in March to expect any miracles.

"There's a saying about the weather here, that Chicago has only two seasons: winter and construction." He laughed.

Rebecca sat back down.

"Since we're pressed for time I've gone ahead and ordered my dinner already. I have another meeting after this one. We're having several strategy meetings here over the next few weeks. In addition to avoiding the distraction of nice weather, meeting here allows us to have some more discussions with PharmaCo at their headquarters in Downers Grove."

Just then their waiter arrived with Rebecca's meal, a salad and a glass of cola. He gave a menu to Dr. Lutkin.

"What is your special today?" Dr. Lutkin asked.

"Chicken a la king."

"I'll have that with some mineral water, please."

The waiter took down his order and walked away.

"I'm going to get right to the point," Rebecca said, completely ignoring her salad. "Our entire industry has come under serious scrutiny in the news. They called us bounty hunters. They called us kidnappers. They said what we did was criminally fraudulent. The others got caught first, so we changed the way we did things. The scandal nearly bankrupted us and we had to restructure for the sake of our shareholders. We believe The Harrison School is well-positioned for strategic restructuring."

She looked down at her salad for the first time and frowned.

"What sort of restructuring did you have in mind?" asked Dr. Lutkin.

Before she answered his question, Rebecca took a sip of her drink and puckered her lips in disgust.

"Here's what I'm thinking. There are several potential growth areas in the troubled teen industry, particularly substance abuse and eating disorders."

She spotted their waiter and waved him over.

"Excuse me, but there's something in my glass that shouldn't be there: one hundred fifty calories. And I also asked to have my salad dressing on the side."

"Oh, I'm so sorry about that. I'll have a new salad and Diet Pepsi for you right away."

"Thank you," Rebecca said firmly.

The waiter took the rejected items and headed toward the kitchen.

"Eating disorders are huge right now. Every girl wants to look like Kate Moss. They're calling it 'heroin chic'. And speaking of heroin, drug rehab is a huge untapped market. With a dual diagnosis of drug or alcohol abuse and mental illness, there is a potential for larger bills.

"I like to think of your facility as the beauty mark on the face of our corporation. Harrison is always the centerfold of our annual report. Whenever they talk about you, senior management always says, 'Let them do whatever they want. They make us look good!' But the past few years have been difficult for us, as you can imagine. We're grateful that your school countered any bad publicity about PHEA during those years."

The waiter came back with Rebecca's drink, salad, and dressing on the side. She stabbed the mixed greens with her fork and staked them to her plate as she meticulously dissected her vegetables with repetitive diagonal cross cuts.

As Rebecca droned on about insurance companies not paying enough and Harrison needing to make more money for PHEA's investors, Dr. Lutkin thought about how easily her makeup could conceal the signs that she was not getting enough nutrition. Her nail polish was holding her brittle fingernails together, and the makeup on her face probably hid the cracked skin at the corners of her mouth, the dark circles around her eyes. Maybe he felt like considering what she might be hiding because he felt so out of place here. Even now, five years after his mentor, Dr. Olmstead, had passed away, being in charge of Harrison still took him by surprise. Shouldn't it be someone else's job to run the school? Sadly there was no one else. Only him. He needed to get his mind back on track and focus on this meeting. Rebecca dipped her fork into the dressing before every bite of salad.

"I have to admit it makes me very uncomfortable looking at our school from an economic perspective. I'm more accustomed to looking at it from a medical perspective," said Dr. Lutkin, noticing the way Rebecca nervously tapped her foot as she ate her salad. "And when I look at it that way, I see very positive results. Forty percent of our patients recover in less than a year. True, there are some who stay with us a little longer, but rarely longer than five years. And per your suggestion, we've recently begun working with more patients who only need brief inpatient treatment. In fact, I just admitted a young man who I expect will likely recover within a month or so. Our methods are working."

"Your methods cost too much," she said coldly.

"Well, what about the agreement we made with PharmaCo? Isn't that at least helping to defray some of our operating costs?"

"That's the only thing that kept you afloat this year, but I don't know if it will last. Frankly, they're unhappy with the way your results compare to theirs."

"I told you, our methods work."

"Yes, but your methods take too long. And you know insurance companies pay far less for therapy than they do for medications."

"So if things go sour with PharmaCo, what are our other options?"

"As I said before, restructure. The Harrison School doesn't have to remain a school. We think it should be a hospital, like all our other facilities. Get them in, get them out, get their money, get them home."

She had finished exactly half of her salad. She put her utensils down on the plate, forming a capital

'X' with the fork and knife.

"Get them home," Dr. Lutkin echoed bitterly. "Did you know that was the general idea behind lobotomies? What you're talking about is the very antithesis of our treatment philosophy. We won't stand for it."

"Then the alternative would be to increase your prices. Of course, you wouldn't be able to treat everybody, but if your methods work as well as you say they do, you can charge for them accordingly."

"If we did that, one year's tuition would cost as much as a year of medical school."

Rebecca covered her plate with her napkin and backed her chair away from the table. There was a sense of finality about the gesture, Dr. Lutkin thought.

"You might not have a choice." She checked her watch. "I've got a meeting with PharmaCo. I have to leave now if I want to get there on time. But you can expect to hear from me again soon. There is still a great deal left for us to discuss."

She stood up and put her coat on, and picked up her cell phone and bag. The coat seemed to overwhelm her, being too loose and not heavy enough for the weather. It made her look small. Dr. Lutkin had treated many patients like her over the years. He felt a wave of compassion rising within him, in spite of everything she'd just said.

"You might find that if you get enough to eat, the cold winters here will be a little easier for you to bear," he said without thinking.

It had just slipped out. He wanted to laugh at himself and all his misgivings about Freudian theories. It was like his slip earlier, "looking at things from a medical perspective." Maybe he couldn't help himself. Maybe it was his only refuge. She stared at him stunned, her secret exposed.

The waiter arrived with Dr. Lutkin's order on a tray.

"Please bring our check. I'll take care of it," said Rebecca, steadying herself and regaining control.

Dr. Lutkin knew that's what it was ultimately about: Rebecca being in control. Even though he didn't have to, he found himself telling her, "There's no need to do that. This one's on me."

It was dark, a night without stars. The sky was tinted an unnatural shade of orange from the streetlamps that lined his grandmother's block. A car pulled up unexpectedly. The windows rolled down. Gunshots erupted from the vehicle without warning or reason. All Devante could do was scream.

He was sitting up in bed now, his shirt drenched with sweat.

Where am I?

This was not his room.

He was dizzy. He curled up into a ball and squeezed his eyes shut, trying to hold on to himself, trying not to let the darkness of this unknown room consume him. He could hear the echo of his pounding heart through the mattress.

In a sudden flash, the light over the bed came on. He jumped up and saw a man standing in the doorway.

"It's okay. Just a bad dream. It's over now." The guy who spoke to him was someone he didn't recognize. "I'm Carlos, one of the night counselors. I heard you from the hallway. You alright?"

Devante shook his head. His heart was pounding and he could hardly catch his breath. He felt like he'd been running too many laps in gym class. Now he knew where he was. Now it was coming back to him. This had been the first time he'd slept in weeks. The last time he slept, he was back at home. And maybe that was where he still expected to wake up.

"You want to talk about it?" Carlos asked.

Devante shook his head again. He couldn't talk about it even if he wanted to. Luckily Carlos seemed to understand.

"That's cool. No problem. Hey, you didn't get to have dinner, did you? You've been asleep all this time. Want to go down to the kitchen and get something to eat?"

Devante nodded. How long had it been since he'd eaten anything? He suddenly felt aware of his long-neglected hunger. His stomach was so empty it ached. He got out of bed and found his shoes beside it, their laces removed. He put them on and left with Carlos.

The kitchen was spacious and its large refrigerator was well-stocked. Carlos let Devante take out the ingredients for a sandwich, though as a precaution, only Carlos could use the knife to slice the tomatoes and turkey. Devante devoured it, feeling hungrier than he ever remembered being in his life. After he'd eaten his fill, he went back to his room, sleepy once again, but too afraid of his nightmares to close his eyes. He spent his entire first night in this state of fitful almost-sleep, grateful for the sunrise the next morning. Carlos sat outside his door the whole time, though Devante had nothing to say to him. Even though he couldn't sleep, it helped to know Carlos was there.

Oddly enough, Devante felt he could sleep once the sun was up. He dozed off for a while. This time he didn't dream at all. He could have stayed like that all day, and would have, but a counselor woke him up.

"You should have some breakfast before your session today," the counselor said. "By the way, I'm Tom."

Tom stood outside the bathroom while Devante showered and dressed. Which was worse: having bars on every window and locks on every door, or having some guy hang around while he brushed his teeth to make sure he didn't try to drown himself? It didn't take a lot of water to drown, he half-remembered from something a scoutmaster or science teacher had said once. How many inches was it again? No, he wouldn't try that. Not today. Or at least not right now.

The glass block walls of the stairwell they walked down reminded him of a kaleidoscope he and his older brother shared when they were little. The light that passed through each pane doused his skin and clothes with patches of color, bright despite the feeble winter sun.

The cafeteria was empty. It reminded him of his past few weeks at home, having the house to himself while his mother took his grandmother to her doctor appointments, or to meetings with aldermen, ministers, neighbors, and anyone else who wanted to save the community as much as she did. Being home alone meant not having to hide in the basement while they thought he was at school. Yet in that silence he had felt the dread that any second something terrible would happen. And now he was starting to feel it again.

"If you're wondering where everyone else is," Tom said, "they're all in their classes and activities already. Next week you'll join them. This week you have a slightly different schedule."

Surprisingly, his breakfast was served on real dishes, and his orange juice was in a real glass. He even ate with metal utensils. And the food they served him was real, too. No mystery meat or chalky powdered eggs like the slop at the hospital. Once he was finished, Tom took his dirty dishes.

"It's almost time for your session. Let's head down to Dr. Lutkin's office now."

As they got closer to Dr. Lutkin's office, Devante could hear music. Jazz. It was familiar yet unfamiliar at the same time. His music teachers were always trying to get him and his friends to listen to more of it, and so was his grandmother. But now he felt like he was hearing it for the first time. The echo in the corridor of lonely saxophones and solitary trumpets made him think of vast wastelands. Or a desert. Or maybe the ruins of some once-great civilization. Desolate music played by the sole survivor of the catastrophe that killed the world. Music that would never have an audience. Or so the last man left had thought.

Actually, he had an audience of one. Dr. Lutkin seemed surprised at the interruption, as though he hadn't been expecting Devante so soon, or else had lost track of time. He got up from his chair and went over to turn off his stereo.

Devante had to say something. He didn't want the music to stop.

"Wait! Don't turn it off."

Dr. Lutkin turned around and looked at Devante. If he was surprised, his face didn't show it.

"You like this music?"

Devante nodded. And then, before he knew it, he was talking again.

"It's lonely. It's like he's the last man left on Earth."

"Would you like to tell me more about that?"

Devante shook his head. He couldn't say another word. He was afraid of what he might feel. He was afraid to feel anything, and afraid to talk about it. And besides, he shouldn't speak. He didn't deserve to. Speaking was a privilege for the living, and he should have been dead. He and Dr. Lutkin both stood there for a moment, the haunting refrain from the record player the only sound filling the silence.

And then Dr. Lutkin said, "You know, I wasn't much older than you when I bought this record. I have some others. Would you like to take a look?"

Devante nodded. He followed Dr. Lutkin over to the little cabinet below the window where he kept his record collection. He looked at the album covers, at the pictures of the men and their instruments, and their names: Thelonious Monk, John Coltrane, Dizzy Gillespie, Charles Mingus, Miles Davis, Dave Brubek, Art Blakey. Some of the names he recognized, others he didn't. Devante chose one that looked interesting and handed it to Dr. Lutkin, who put it on the turntable and played it for him.

Devante sat on the floor beside one of the speakers. He wanted to lose himself in the music, but instead he was finding emotions he'd kept hidden from himself. There were some feelings, he thought, that couldn't be put into words. But there were musical notes for them. And melodies, and harmonies, and chords. He had hoped to remain as numb as he was wordless, but somehow the music wouldn't let him. Rather than feeling numb, he was feeling the vibrations of the music as it resonated in the speakers, in his ears, in his heart. He stared intently at the record as it turned.

Dr. Lutkin pulled up a chair and sat beside him, letting Devante choose new records and playing them for him. Before long, fifty minutes had passed.

He looked at his watch and told Devante they were out of time. But before Devante could go, there was something he had to say. Maybe it was okay, only for now, to say it.

"When I listen to music, that's the only time I don't feel numb inside."

Dr. Lutkin seemed pleased.

"You know, we have a music room with a piano. I understand you used to play?"

Devante nodded.

"There's someone waiting outside my office who can show it to you."

Dr. Lutkin opened the door to reveal a lone girl standing expectantly. Her two long braids were held together at the ends with plastic flower barrettes, and she reminded him of one of the artsy kids from his school. The dress she wore looked like something out of a picture book, like she was Gretel, that girl who was lost in the forest with her brother. She wore a jean jacket over it and some brown combat boots. They laced all the way up to her knees. He'd never thought of shoelaces as a status symbol before, but he was jealous. The way his unlaced Doc Martens flopped around on his feet was almost comical.

"Devante, I'd like you to meet Janina. Janina, this is Devante."

"Hi," Janina said shyly.

So his name is Devante, Janina thought. She liked it.

Gail had watched as the door to the office opened and
Dr. Lutkin walked out with a patient, a tall, lanky,
African-American boy with haunted eyes. And even
though the boy looked nothing like him, Gail found
herself thinking of her brother and felt a sharp pang
of sadness. A girl who had been sitting in the waiting
area with Gail had gotten up and walked nervously
over to them. Though the girl was quiet, her outfit
definitely made a statement. Whatever this girl's
troubles were, she certainly knew how to express
herself, Gail thought. It was nice to see that the
patients were allowed to wear their own clothes here,
and weren't limited to pajamas like so many of the
teens at Haven House. Wearing one's own clothing
there was a privilege that had to be earned.

Something she'd read recently came to mind,
that a Black child with emotional problems was more
likely to end up in the justice system than in a

treatment setting. Gail was glad to see two of them who were getting help. At Haven House, all of her patients had been White.

Gail sat in an exquisite wingback chair in the lobby outside Dr. Lutkin's office. It was upholstered in a colorful fabric that looked like it could have been hand-painted. And maybe it was. Its mate was similar, but not identical. Instead of a coffee table, there was a large sturdy-legged ottoman covered in fabric similar to the kind on the chairs. The vibrant chandelier overhead looked like it belonged in a modern art museum. She'd never seen anything like it before. The rug beneath her feet reminded her of some of the beautiful fabrics Anjali had brought back from India last summer. The copper reception desk curved forward like a smile.

On the outside, the building looked like a castle. Not a whimsical theme park castle like the one at Disneyland, but one with real historical character, like the ones she'd visited during her college semester abroad in Europe. But she couldn't let its looks deceive her. She couldn't allow herself to be misled by appearances, as she'd been at Haven House. After all, Haven House had a nice lobby, too.

But the rest of Haven House had ugly institutional furniture that looked like something out of a prison. The sofas had ripped cushions that were duct-taped back together. The furniture there didn't just withstand abuse. It seemed to ask for it. And twice while she had been there, the glass top of the coffee table in the lobby had been shattered by furious new patients who had been brought there against their will.

Once Dr. Lutkin had introduced the two teens to each other, they walked down the hallway together. After he'd seen them off, Dr. Lutkin waved at Gail from his doorway.

"Please come in!"

Gail walked through the open door and had a seat in front of Dr. Lutkin's desk. His office was decorated in deep, rich jewel tones: amethyst purples, sapphire blues, emerald greens. The chair she sat in now rivaled the one in the lobby, both in comfort and in style. There was a large rug on the floor of the office with a bold modern geometric pattern on it. It reminded her of jazz for some reason. Dr. Lutkin shook her hand.

"So nice to meet you. Charlotte—I mean Dr. Hoffman—has told me so much about you."

Gail tried not to cringe as she wondered what Dr. Hoffman had told him.

"It's nice to meet you as well."

When he sat down behind his desk, Dr. Lutkin seemed shorter. Gail realized that the seat of his chair was lower than hers. It probably put him at eye level with his young patients and made him seem less intimidating to them. She noticed a plaque on his desk. Engraved on a brass plate was a quotation:

...the only people for me are the mad ones, the ones

who are mad to live, mad to talk, mad to be saved...
—Jack Kerouac

An interesting choice for a psychiatrist, she thought.

"I should add that Dr. Hoffman spoke highly of you, which probably sounds surprising given her teaching style," said Dr. Lutkin, as if he'd read her mind. "I understand you're a resident in psychiatry?"

Now came the moment she'd been dreading. Once again, she'd have to explain herself.

"I was until a few weeks ago. I never thought I'd end up leaving seven months into it, but I had to. I couldn't take it anymore. The attitude of the staff at the hospital I worked at before was punitive, not therapeutic. They saw the patients as bad kids who needed someone to teach them a lesson."

Dr. Lutkin nodded.

"Sadly, it seems that in our mental health care system, we've set up regulations to benefit administrators and staff at the expense of the patients. And that was why when I was just starting out in my psychiatry practice, I was delighted to help my old professor, Dr. Olmsted, found this school. Its design is based on our treatment philosophies, some of which we borrowed from Bruno Bettelheim and his Orthogenic School at the University of Chicago. Others we developed on our own from research or learned from trial and error. Let me show you around and tell you more."

As they went back out into the lobby, he told her about the school in numbers: forty residential students, twenty teens and twenty children under twelve, half girls, half boys, and an experienced staff of counselors, social workers, psychiatrists, psychologists, teachers, and nurses to help all of them.

The hallway leading to the rest of the school had a beautiful mural painted on it. A midnight blue sky brightened by a smiling moon gradually faded into a light blue sky illuminated by a smiling sun. Stars danced in the night sky and birds frolicked in its sun-drenched counterpart. And beneath those skies was a city of buildings of various sizes, full of little people going about their daily lives. At the very bottom of the mural along the baseboard was an elegantly painted quote in bold cursive letters:

"Even the darkest night will end and the sun will rise."

— Victor Hugo, *Les Misérables*

Gail and Dr. Lutkin passed some students who were headed to their afternoon therapy sessions.

"Most facilities are too poorly designed to help anyone. I believe that within every patient there is an innate drive toward maturity and wholeness, and being in an environment like this stimulates positive growth."

Dr. Lutkin explained that the story of the school's furnishings was the story of Dr. Olmsted.

Many years ago the building that now housed The Harrison School had been a small hotel. The Olmsted family had been in the hotel business, and Dr. Olmsted's father was surprised when his son became a psychiatrist. The building of a new expressway and medical center nearby had caused a sharp decline in business that led to the hotel's closing. It no longer seemed so luxurious with the wail of sirens and roar of traffic all around it. It had sat vacant for nearly a decade before Dr. Olmsted decided to found The Harrison School, named for the street it was on. He hired the top-notch interior designers his family had worked with for years to create the school's healing environment. The money left by his parents helped pay for all of it. When Dr. Olmsted died five years ago, he left all his money in a trust for the school.

Every element of the school's design had been carefully chosen. The meticulously crafted furniture was meant to instill a sense of self-worth in patients. But there was no uniformity. Instead, there was a mix of old and new furniture, and styles from all over the world. Still, everything looked good together even though it didn't always match.

"We chose colors and patterns that are upbeat, though we are careful how we use them. Red, for example, can feel too aggressive. Black is stylish and modern but it can be too severe. And stripes can look too much like prison bars and feel confining." Guiding Gail through another corridor, Dr. Lutkin said, "We have given special attention to transitional spaces like our stairwells and hallways, because therapy is a period of transition."

As Gail listened to him speak, she had a hard time placing his accent. Just when she thought Dr. Lutkin might be from the West Coast, he'd pronounce a word in a way that made her think he might be from the East Coast. Other times his words had a Midwestern flavor. Usually she had a good ear for accents, but maybe Dr. Lutkin had moved around a lot.

They walked by a classroom with a big window. A group therapy session was about to begin. Six teenagers sat in a semicircle in front of a chalkboard where their therapist was writing, "What gives your life meaning?"

"All the students here have group sessions every afternoon," Dr. Lutkin explained. "It gives them an environment where they feel accepted."

He led her up a staircase painted in cheerful colors and into a large room where younger children were playing. Many of them didn't interact with each other. A few seemed perplexed and stared into space. Once again Gail thought about her brother, remembering what he was like as a little boy.

"We have a few cases of childhood schizophrenia. It's such a difficult diagnosis, both for the children and their parents. But we hope that, with early intervention and education tailored to their individual needs, we can help them."

"Early intervention is a lifesaver," Gail agreed, hoping her sadness didn't show on her face.

The boy and girl Gail had seen earlier walked past them.

Once they were out of earshot, Dr. Lutkin said, "Being able to help him gives her the feeling that she has something to offer."

That was a surprising perspective. At Haven House, the kids were not allowed to touch each other and boys were kept as far away from girls as possible. The usual social interactions Gail would have expected amongst teenagers were hindered by these rules. It seemed that their anxieties and awkwardness were only made worse by them. Even a pat on the back or a friendly hug was considered an infraction worthy of the dreaded chair therapy.

"All we ask of them is that they follow a few simple rules, namely that they respect each other and the staff enough to tell the truth and not make fun of each other's conditions, that they help each other, and that they don't use alcohol, tobacco, or drugs while they're here. None of them are admitted unless they want to be here, and none of them have a history of violent behavior. In order for our methods to work, these are the conditions we need."

Gail was impressed. This place seemed like the real deal. There was nice furniture in every room, not just in areas where the parents would see it. There were no bars on the windows because they locked electronically. Dr. Lutkin only had to unlock a few of the doors. He told her that some of the decorations and artwork were created by the students in art therapy, like the napkin rings on the tables in the cafeteria. And everywhere Gail looked, there had been counselors working with kids. Most of the counselors were close to her age or maybe a few years younger. Dr. Lutkin said many of them were graduate students, mainly studying psychology or social work. The whole environment was infused with positive energy. This was the kind of place where a troubled kid could get well.

Gail thanked Dr. Lutkin at the end of the tour.

"This is the most impressive facility I've ever seen," she told him.

"Thank you. Our counseling staff is a very important part of creating our supportive environment. This position calls for deep personal involvement and commitment. That's why I evaluate every applicant based on who they are as a person, not just by what degrees and certifications they have. So far, I think you'd be a good fit, but I'd like to have you come back for a second interview. Are you available on Friday?"

Gail happily said yes.

At the same time they were touring the school, so was Rebecca Galt. In fact, she gave her boss, Peter Roark, her own tour. She showed him the single bedrooms the teens slept in—wasted space, big enough to hold three or even four patients each. They had designer décor, wasted on kids who were too out of touch with reality to notice their surroundings. There were counselors everywhere, a waste of money. Why pay them to supervise the kids when locks and bars were less expensive than all those salaries? And the cafeteria, which still bore traces of the elegant hotel restaurant it had once been, was perhaps one of the most wasteful features of all. Rebecca and Peter watched the kitchen staff setting the tables for dinner, outraged by the ceramic dishes they served the food on, not to mention the high quality of the food itself. Couldn't Harrison just use canned and frozen ingredients like all their other facilities? Did they really need fresh fruits and vegetables? Did they have to have cloth napkins with hand-painted napkin rings?

Peter pointed through the doorway at two unaccompanied Black teens in the corridor, a girl with two long braids and a boy with floppy ankle boots.

"Look at those two," Peter shook his head. "They should be locked in their rooms, just like the rest of them, just like we do things at Haven House."

CHAPTER 9
THE MYSTERY BOY

"And this is the music room," Janina said as she led Devante to a large room next to the cafeteria. "We have some guitars, drums, and a few other instruments, and of course the piano. Do you know how to play? I don't."

Devante stepped up to the piano. He looked like he might sit down and play, but he didn't. Instead, he moved his hands so lightly across the keyboard that the piano didn't make a sound. Janina admired his long, handsome fingers. He probably did know how to play, she thought.

Devante backed away from the piano and put his hands into his pockets. He was afraid that the feeling of his fingers on the keys would make him start to remember things he was trying to forget.

Since Janina had already showed him the art room, she decided to stop by occupational therapy. Today it was being held in the kitchen. She wondered what her classmates were making. Something smelled good. Two counselors watched as Marcia, Ed, and a few other kids mixed cookie dough. Ed was obsessively lining up perfectly formed balls of dough on a cookie sheet, wearing gloves as usual. It was a slow and methodical process. Marcia looked like she was getting impatient. Janina could imagine how she must feel. In the time it took Ed to get the dough on the cookie sheet, the cookies could have been baked and ready.

"Ed, are you still trying to make the perfect cookie?"

"Yes, but certain people keep getting in my way." He glared at Marcia.

Janina felt bad for Marcia. The only time Janina was paired with Ed and they tried making cookies together, it had ended in tears. She had a very hard time with perfectionists. It was too much like being back at her old school. Still, she was glad that Marcia was there to see Devante with her own eyes. When Janina had told Marcia about him last night, before she knew his name, they had called him the mystery boy.

"Does this mystery boy of yours really exist?" Marcia had asked.

"Of course he does!" Janina had insisted. "I'm not making this up."

"If he's not real, it's okay. You know, my sister Jan had an imaginary boyfriend once. She told us his name was George Glass." Marcia had said with a little laugh.

But now Janina was getting the last laugh. She

turned to Devante. "The cookies will probably be ready by the time I'm finished showing you around. Chocolate chip is my favorite. What about you?"

She didn't expect him to answer, but he nodded as if he was saying, "Mine, too." Words were still too much for him to manage, other than what he'd said in Dr. Lutkin's office. Devante felt safe talking to him, but not anyone else. Not yet. But this girl seemed nice enough. He didn't want to leave the aroma of the baking cookies behind, but he followed Janina as she led the way. She showed him the conservatory where an indoor garden was growing. That was occupational therapy too, Janina had explained. Then they went up to the second floor where there were younger kids. Devante had never thought about children that small going crazy. Then they went upstairs to the third floor and she took him to the girls' wing, where Nurse Erica started following them immediately.

"And this is my room," said Janina as she opened the door.

He followed her in. The nurse stood right outside. Janina was nervous. This was the first time a boy had ever been in her room. She hadn't wanted the other boys to visit, but Devante was different.

The first thing he noticed was the paper flowers. They were everywhere. It seemed like there were hundreds of them on Janina's wall, and even hanging from her ceiling on strands of green yarn that looked like vines. There were big ones and small ones in every color of the rainbow. And so were the paper butterflies. The glitter on their wings sparkled in the afternoon sunlight.

"I made them myself, in art therapy," Janina said proudly.

Devante didn't say anything to her, but he smiled. And Janina smiled back. He looked around some more. There were some drawings taped to the other wall, really good ones. She had the same furniture he did. The covers on her bed looked like she'd brought them from home. They were as colorful as her flowers and the outfit she wore. There were more flowers drawn on a sign taped over her headboard that said, in elaborate hand drawn script, "What angel wakes me from my flowery bed?"

Then he saw her white Snuggle Bear. And he saw drops of blood raining down on it. The blood formed a steady trickle, then gushed down the pillows, over the comforter, spilling on the floor.

He screamed as he ran down the hallway. In his mind, the hallway was no longer a hallway. He was outside on the sidewalk. He was trying to hide. There was gunfire. There were shots. He didn't want to get hit. He couldn't protect her. So much blood. Blood on the roses. Blood on the teddy bear. Blood on his jeans. Blood on his hands! But it wasn't his blood. It was hers. The wrong place at the wrong time—

"It's alright, Devante. You're safe here."

He looked up. Now he was in the hallway again and the nurse was speaking to him. Her voice was calming. He looked at his hands, no longer covered in blood.

It's over. I'm in a safe place, he thought.

The nurse was looking at him. Did she know what he had seen just then? Did she know how crazy he was?

"I'm going to take you back to your room. You can stay there until dinner, okay?"

CHAPTER 10

TO HIDE THE HEART THAT BLEEDS

Janina stood staring at Devante and Nurse Erica in disbelief. She had no idea why he fled the room. Meredith had seen what just happened.

"It's not your fault," she told Janina. "He must have been triggered by something."

Janina watched as Nurse Erica led Devante out of the girls' wing.

"You mean, like, a flashback?" she asked. She'd known kids who'd had flashbacks before.

"Yes," Meredith said.

Janina wondered what he'd seen that would have made him have a flashback. It couldn't have been her teddy bear. Why would anyone be afraid of that? She hadn't expected their time together to be cut so short. Sure, she'd been warned that he didn't talk, but she hoped that maybe he might. Just to her. Meredith told Janina it was okay for her to go to the art room if she wanted.

Philip, the art teacher, was still there, and so was a boy named Leon. He was working on the cover of his goodbye book. It was a school tradition: an autograph book the other kids could sign since he was leaving. She hadn't seen Leon around that much. He was in the transitional group now, which meant he no longer spent the night at Harrison or went to classes there. He only came for therapy. He was almost ready to leave for good. Janina wondered when she would be.

She had about a half hour until her mood disorders group, so she found a big blank canvas and started on a new painting.

I want to paint some flowers, she thought. *I want them to be the color of a thousand screaming suns.*

She wanted to paint something as bright as her heart felt for that brief moment when Devante had smiled at her.

The half hour passed too quickly. She took one last look at her shockingly bright canvas before she went to her group therapy session, a little sad that she had to leave it. But she could work on it again tomorrow.

That night, Janina was glad to have Devante at the dinner table with her, even though he didn't speak. After dinner, he even sat next to her on one of the couches in the lounge while she sketched. He didn't know it, but she was drawing a picture of him. There was something sort of comforting about his silence. Somehow it made it easier to talk to him. It freed her from her usual self-consciousness. She told him more about the school, and a little about herself, but never asked him any questions.

It was good that she didn't pressure him to talk. He didn't know what he'd tell her anyway. He wasn't ready to say anything about why he was there, or even about his flashback earlier. After it was over and the nurse had brought him back to his room, he had sat and stared at the wall for a while until Tom had come and asked him if he wanted to sit in the lounge until dinner. He had sunk down into one of the huge beanbag chairs and stared for a long time at a painting with a lot of circles in it. No one ever tried to make him talk.

People here weren't like his parents, begging or demanding that he say something. He was still getting used to the idea of being here, but what did that mean? Just how crazy was he, really? His teachers had always told him how smart he was and had complimented his mind. His Grandma had said he had a mind like a steel trap because his memory was so good. He felt like he could memorize anything. But now what he once thought was a blessing felt like a curse. He could no longer trust his mind and he could no longer bear his memories.

Before he came here, he had tried so hard to pretend that everything was okay. He had found ways to hide it. Too scared to go outside after dark, he took the trash out during the day instead. Too afraid of his nightmares to sleep at night, he decided to stay up. No longer having an appetite but not wanting to waste the food his grandma cooked, he offered to do the dishes and hid his leftovers in the deep freezer in the basement. Unable to cope with school again, he stayed home. Not wanting his mother to have anything else to worry about, he agreed to go back to school last Friday. And maybe if it wasn't for that picture of Monica and that couple he saw in the hall that morning...he thought about that day too much. Maybe he should tell Dr. Lutkin about it.

"I wanted to talk to you about what happened right before I came here. I mean, right before the overpass," he said to him at the beginning of their session the next day. "I keep wondering what it would be like if things had gone differently. I mean, if I hadn't tried to jump. Do you think I could've gone back to school? Do you think I could've kept pretending to be normal?"

"What do you mean by normal?"

"Acting like it never happened and everything's okay."

"Do you really think, after what happened, that it would be normal to act like everything was still the same?"

His mother had. It had made her want to work harder, she'd told him. Ever since they moved in with Grandma she'd talked about building a community center. Now she wanted to name it after Monica. His friends didn't talk about it, either. Chad and Jerome had been close to Monica, too, but ever since it happened, they'd been avoiding him. And after the police had brought him to the hospital, his father told him that he had to go back to his office to work on something after he'd only been there for a few minutes. Now that he thought of it, no one was acting normal. He wondered if he'd ever feel normal again, or what the word even meant anymore.

What was normal? He thought about it all day. Was it normal for him to be in his room sleeping—or trying to, anyway—while everyone else was in their classes? And who was acting normal? Take dinner, for example. Kathleen ate everything with her hands, even her salad. Meanwhile, Ed was going over his silverware like a health inspector. And when Nurse Erica came around with medicine for them to take, Marcia held up her little paper cup of pills and said, "Cheers!" Then everyone at their table joined in. He did too, reluctantly. The pills left a bitter aftertaste.

Devante could still taste them after dinner, while he sat beside Janina on a couch in the lounge. She showed him a book she was reading.

"I just got it for my birthday. Even though it's old, it's new to me. And I found this poem I really like. Can I read it to you?"

Devante nodded.

"The title of the poem is 'From The Dark Tower' and it's by Countee Cullen.

We were not made eternally to weep.
The night whose sable breast relieves the stark,

White stars is no less lovely being dark,
And there are buds that cannot bloom at all
In light, but crumple, piteous, and fall;
So in the dark we hide the heart that bleeds,
And wait, and tend our agonizing seeds."

He liked the part about the stars, and about hiding "the heart that bleeds." That's what he had done. That's what he was still trying to do. He thought of it that night as he lay in bed, fighting the need to sleep. Closing his eyes meant surrendering to whatever nightmares his tortured mind could conjure. But it was too late now. It was almost time for lights out.

Though he felt immature for thinking of it, he wished he had a nightlight. He could never bring himself to ask for one. Wasn't he too old to be afraid of the dark?

Janina would be going to bed soon herself. But first, she had to write something down. Reading from the book Dr. Lutkin had given her inspired her to write a poem of her own.

What do you dream of, caramel boy,
when you descend into your slumber?
I dream about you and your eyes of burnt umber.
Do you ever dream of me, caramel boy,
and what we could do together?
I dream about you & I

always & forever.
Why do you smile at me, caramel boy,
with your pretty chocolate eyes?

She had to think of something good to rhyme with "eyes" and it was too late to go look it up in the rhyming dictionary. So the rest of her poem would have to wait.

While Janina drifted off to sleep, Devante cowered in the oppressive darkness of his room. The orange glow of the streetlights outside gave him no comfort. He couldn't look out of his window. He couldn't close his eyes, either. There would be nightmares. He was sure of it. So he went out to the hallway to see if Carlos was there. He was, sitting in a chair and reading a book.

"Can't sleep?"

Devante shook his head. "Nightmares. Constantly," Devante sighed.

He was starting to find the words again, and feeling less afraid of saying them.

"If you ever decide you want to talk about them, I'm here," said Carlos.

"Thanks."

Nights like this when he was still at home, he'd mute his TV and play video games until dawn, stacking the Tetris blocks on each other over and over again. Somehow he had found it soothing. He couldn't play any of his war games anymore. He couldn't stand to see the guns. But Carlos explained that it was too late to play video games in the lounge. Devante was supposed to be in his room.

"But if you don't tell anyone," Carlos whispered, "you can borrow this."

He took a Game Boy out of his backpack. He had a few different games for it, including Tetris. Devante played until both he and the Game Boy's batteries were drained. He woke up from another nightmare just as the sun was coming up. Soon it would be time for Carlos to go. Devante gave the Game Boy back to him.

"You get any sleep?" he asked Devante.

"A couple hours, I think. You know, it's easier for me to just sleep during the day."

"Going nocturnal? Be careful. It messes up your internal clock. Trust me."

But it was clear from the look in Devante's weary eyes that he needed to rest.

"Tell you what. I'll let Tom know that you need to sleep in again today."

"Thanks."

"But you've got to promise me you'll talk to Dr. Lutkin about this. You need to get enough sleep, okay?"

Devante nodded. He went back into his room and laid down. He felt exhausted, yet still afraid of having another nightmare. He laid there for the next two hours with his eyes closed, right on the verge of sleep, but never actually going to it. Then Tom came and said he needed to shower and dress for his session with Dr. Lutkin. And suddenly Devante remembered he hadn't eaten, either. His appetite was starting to come back. He was glad there was enough time for a quick bowl of cold cereal.

Dr. Lutkin noticed his exhaustion right away.

"How have you been sleeping lately?" he asked him.

"I can't. I have nightmares, and other times I wake up screaming. My own voice wakes me up, but I don't even know what I was screaming about."

"Those are called night terrors."

"That's a good name for them. I wish I could stop feeling so afraid all the time."

"Tell me some of the things you're afraid of."

"I can't talk about it now." He panicked. "Please, can't we talk about something else?"

"Sure. I'm not going to push you. You can tell me when you're ready. You said something interesting in your first session. You told me that Miles Davis sounded like he was the last man on Earth. Would you feel comfortable explaining what you meant by that?"

"Okay."

Dr. Lutkin put the record on, as if to refresh Devante's memory.

"It made me think about a guy who's the only survivor of some huge worldwide disaster," Devante said as the song played. "And he feels so guilty about it. Why did he survive when the others died? And if he's really the last one left, how is he supposed to go on? What is he supposed to do?"

"And how do you think you can relate to his

story?"

"That's how I feel. It's how I've felt ever since... you know." Devante sank hopelessly into his chair. "I feel different from other people. It's like I'm cut off from everyone else and old before my time. I feel like I'll never have a normal life again. Or a future."

"Now I know you're crazy."

Alejandra had made sure the counselors couldn't hear what she was saying to Janina as they walked to class.

"Your new boyfriend doesn't even talk!" Alejandra laughed. Name-calling wasn't allowed here, but it was her favorite rule to break.

"Mind your own business. He's not my boyfriend!"

Of course, Janina wished he was. They'd just had lunch together. Devante looked like he was about to say something to her for the first time, but he didn't. And the disappointment was crushing. And what could Alejandra possibly know about it? It was hard to concentrate on writing her book report with Alejandra's words echoing in her mind. Why was Alejandra always telling Janina she wasn't really crazy? And who asked her, anyway? Janina had planned to make a beautiful cover page for her report, but now she didn't feel like it. She was sad and angry and frustrated. She could never think of snappy comebacks when people teased her. Not right away. A clever retort would always come to mind a week later, and by then whoever was teasing her had found some new reason to pick on her. Her delayed reaction would just give them one more reason to make fun of her.

All this time, she'd been staring out the window without even realizing it. The sky was white and blank. It sure looked cold out there. At her old school, staring out of windows during class was one of the many things she used to get in trouble for. Just the thought of it made her feel like crying.

"Are you alright?" Matthew, her teacher asked.

From across the room, Alejandra watched to see how much damage she'd done, and whether Janina would rat on her.

"Just thinking about some things," Janina said.

"Take all the time you need," said Matthew. "And if you need to talk to one of the counselors or Dr. Lutkin about it, let me know."

She thought of what Dr. Lutkin was always telling her, that she shouldn't be so hard on herself all the time. She knew it in her head, but still didn't feel it in her heart. Why did she have to be so weird? Why couldn't she just be normal? Why couldn't she fit in? She was too sensitive. Things that bothered her would never bother other kids, at least not the ones outside this school. She wasn't good at standing up for herself, or getting back at the kids who made fun of her. Did that really matter?

So what if Alejandra's good at making fun of people? She can't draw like me, Janina thought.

She found some heavy drawing paper and some oil pastels, and started on her book report cover. She spent so much time working on it that she never actually finished the report itself.

"Good work so far," Matthew encouraged her. "You can finish the rest of it in class tomorrow."

There were no bells when their classes ended. It would have been too startling and disruptive, Dr. Lutkin had told her when she asked about it. Now that she was out of class for the day, it was time for her second mood disorders group meeting of the week. For once, she had a reason to feel good about it since Devante was there.

When Janina walked in, Devante noticed that she was the only one in the room with shoelaces. Everyone else's shoes buckled or were the slip-on kind, or were unlaced, like his. He wondered what it meant. Then Zack's voice interrupted his thoughts.

"Let me guess. You tried to jump," he said to Devante.

His jaw dropped. How did Zack know?

This was a morbid little game Zack played whenever he got there early and a new kid was joining the group. It didn't have a name, but in Janina's head she called it "Guess the Method." For some of them, it was obvious, scars on the wrists, for example. Trying to hide them didn't work. Zack always said extra-long sleeves or lots of big bracelets were a dead giveaway. For others, the scars were invisible. But everyone in the group had their reasons to be there. Everyone in the group had some form of depression. A few were bipolar, meaning that when they weren't depressed, they were manic and restless. Valerie and Scott, the therapists in charge of the group, had subtle ways of getting newcomers to open up. Zack's way of doing it was more like ripping off a Band-Aid. Or picking at a scab.

"Leave him alone, Zack!" Janina protested.

"Leave him alone, Zack!" Alejandra mimicked her, not realizing Valerie and Scott were coming through the door behind her. "Isn't it sweet of her to stand up for her boyfriend like that?"

"There'll be no teasing, Alejandra," said Valerie firmly.

She took a seat. Scott noticed Devante.

"Everyone, we have a new member of our group. Rather than giving the new guy a hard time, let's have someone who's been here a while go first." He turned and looked at Alejandra. "Alejandra, I know you've been dealing with some challenges this week. How's that been going?"

"Okay, I guess," she said softly, looking at the floor. "It's always been easier to cut myself than tell people how I really feel. I just get so overwhelmed by my feelings sometimes. I'm so afraid that when my depression comes back, it'll just sweep me away and drown me. I know it's coming! I just have to be stronger. And I'm really trying. I'm being as strong as I can be. I hope it's enough."

Devante looked at her and nodded. He knew exactly what she meant.

"That was good, Alejandra," said Valerie. "Does anyone want to comment on what she just said?"

Janina was afraid to say what she just realized, but said it anyway. Valerie and Scott made it easier to do that.

"I know you're trying to be stronger, but you don't have to make fun of people to do it. I mean, is that why you keep making fun of me?"

"I don't know why I do that."

"Janina, I know that was hard for you to say, and I'm glad you're speaking up for yourself. Now can you tell Alejandra how you feel about what she does?"

"I feel ashamed of myself. I feel like crying. I wonder if people are laughing at me behind my back. And I feel like I'll never be normal."

Her voice wavered, and Devante wondered if she was about to cry. So far she wasn't. But he could definitely relate to what she'd said about feeling like she'd never be normal. Maybe he wasn't totally alone after all. After they helped Alejandra and Janina work things out, Scott and Valerie tried to get him to say something to the group. But it was still too overwhelming. And then there was what Zack said when he first came in. Had everyone in there tried to kill themselves? Even Janina?

Devante hadn't thought much about that before, about why Janina was there. Then again, he'd been so caught up in his own problems that he hadn't thought much about why anyone was there, other than those little kids he'd seen the other day. He wondered how many of them had seen things they were too young to see and weren't ready to deal with. It was hard enough to deal with what he had been through at fifteen, but what if he'd only been five? He thought about it all through dinner, as he sat across from Janina. His thoughts made it hard for him to eat. He sliced his turkey burger down the middle and moved his vegetables aimlessly across his plate.

Why was life so unfair? Why was he safe inside this building when there were kids in Grandma's neighborhood who would never be? And what had they done to deserve that? His mother had started calling the neighborhood an inner city battleground, just as bad as Bosnia or the Persian Gulf. Dr. Lutkin had told him that for centuries soldiers had come back from wars with the same stress disorder he had. But he wasn't a soldier, just a kid, caught in the middle of someone else's war, and he felt like he didn't deserve to have survived it.

Janina looked across the table at him, noticing that the napkin ring he had was one of the ones she had painted. It seemed like a good sign somehow. She encouraged him to try his turkey burger, and he was glad he did. He even finished most of it, despite being so consumed by his thoughts that he imagined that sad

Miles Davis song playing in his head. On the way back upstairs, Janina walked beside him, wishing she knew what was on his mind.

"I was gonna ask if you'd like to play Connect Four with me, but you look like something's bothering you," she said when they got back to the lounge. "Anyway, if you want to play, I'll be sitting at this table."

He slumped down in the seat across from hers, thinking she was smart to pick a game that didn't involve talking. What was the point of saying anything if he didn't even deserve to live? Why was he still here, anyway? Maybe he could tell her how bad he felt. Maybe she would understand. She might have felt that way, too.

And so he looked at her and said, "I wish I could erase myself."

She was stunned. It was the first time she had heard his voice, and he was saying such a terrible thing.

"Could you draw a picture of me so I could erase it?"

Her face felt hot all of a sudden. She remembered the drawing she had done a few days ago. How could she erase the wonderful pencil lines that formed his face? She picked up her sketchbook and slowly turned back the pages until she found it. Then she showed it to him.

"I already drew a picture of you."

When she looked at him, she saw a

masterpiece. It was a shame he didn't see it.

"You think I look like that?"

What he saw on that sheet of paper was nothing at all like the face he saw in the mirror through his sleep-starved eyes. She had captured something about him that he never noticed before, something good.

"I could never erase you."

He looked at her, then back at her drawing again. He felt like somehow she had managed to get to know him, even though this was the first time they'd had a real conversation. He didn't know what to say, but he did like the drawing. He could at least tell her that.

"You're a dope artist."

"Thanks." She smiled.

"And I changed my mind. I don't want you to erase it."

"I'm glad you don't, 'cause I spent a lot of time on it."

"Can I see your other drawings?" he said with a tentative finger on the corner of the sketchbook.

"Sure. They're mostly sketches, though," she explained.

A drawing book she'd been reading had suggested doing sketches of everyday things like hallways and furniture. She thought it was good practice for her graphic novel so she could make the backgrounds look realistic. Looking at her sketches made her want to work on *Psindrome* a little bit more.

While Devante was looking at her sketchbook, she picked up from where she left off.

The kids from Unit A were huddled together in front of the Chicago Juvenile Psychiatric Institute, where they'd been standing ever since they evacuated the building for the fire alarm. They told the angry orderlies that they weren't leaving until they found out what happened to Steffanie and Tevin. Josefina had threatened to burn the whole place down if they didn't comply. For once, the staff was starting to believe she truly had the power of pyrokinesis.

"They're scared 'cause Steffanie and Tevin know too much about the conspiracy! First they fluoridate our water, then they make us take radioactive pills. Are they gonna send their aliens to abduct us next?"

"Last night in my sleep I was visited by a series of aliens in white coats," Natasha told them. "They looked into my head and saw what I was thinking! They used their machines."

"Who are they?" Carlton asked her.

"You mean like the 'they' that is responsible for the thought control?" asked Slater. "The 'they' who still won't tell us about the alien autopsy? How about their Spam conspiracy? They have an international plot against me and I don't even know who THEY are!"

"I can see her." Natasha pointed at a ghostly figure looming in the distance.

It was Steffanie! She had finally found a way to astral project herself so that the other kids could see her too, even if they weren't psychic like Natasha.

"He's locked us in the basement!" she told her horrified fellow patients.

"What are you working on?" asked Devante.

"My graphic novel." She put her pen down and showed it to him.

But before he could read it, the counselors told them it was time to go back to their rooms and get ready for bed.

"You can see it tomorrow," she told him.

"That's what's up. I really like your art." He smiled at her.

On her way back to her room, she couldn't stop smiling. Maybe he would be her boyfriend after all. But when she looked at herself in the mirror and saw her braids, she frowned. She had always felt like her hair wasn't really hers, but her mother's. After all, Mama was the hair expert. She was the one who knew just how to wash and blow dry it bone straight, without ever needing to use a relaxer or a pressing comb. Even now, when she came to visit her at school, Mama washed and dried it for her. Janina's hair had been Mama's business card. She was her mother's model. And Mama told all her clients the story of how she sought out the expertise of Egyptian and Dominican hairdressers at the hair shows she went to so she could learn their special blow drying technique since her little girl was too tender-headed for hot combs and chemicals.

After school and on the weekends, Mama would proudly show her clients Janina's head full of beautiful virgin hair that had never once been straightened with a chemical relaxer. When Janina came to the Harrison school, she didn't know what to do with her hair without Mama there to help her every day. Because she had always daydreamed while Mama did her hair, Janina had never learned how to style it. So she put it in braids. Two braids with a center part. Two braids like a little girl. Sometimes she would tuck the ends of the braids back into her ponytail holders, forming a sort of teardrop shape with each one. Other times she would coil her two braids into buns and the kids who were *Star Wars* fans said they made her look like Princess Leia. She thought the two buns looked like the ears of a teddy bear. Those three hairstyles were the only ones in her repertoire. She had never tried anything else. Mama was a tough act to follow.

Now she realized it was time for a new look. She was tired of wearing her hair like a little girl. So she took the barrettes off, undid her braids, and combed it out. It wasn't a fancy style, like Mama would have done. She wasn't sure if it looked good enough. But she kind of liked it. The braids had given her hair soft waves. Her new style made her feel pretty. She decided that from now on, she would braid her hair at night to keep the waves, then comb it out in the morning.

She turned and looked at her bed. There was Snuggle.

"I don't know how I should say this to you, baby, but it's over," she said to her teddy bear. "Oh, don't give me that pitiful look! This is very hard for me, too. I've spent some of the best years of my life with you, Snuggle Bear. But after all the many nights I've spent with you in my arms and all the places we've gone together, I've met somebody new."

She picked Snuggle up and put him in the bottom drawer of her dresser.

From her winter emergency room rotation, Gail had learned that in Chicago the cold was a force to be reckoned with. She had treated patients with frostbite, hypothermia, broken bones from slipping and falling on slippery sidewalks, some who had heart attacks after shoveling snow, and even a few who were unfortunate enough to have chunks of ice crash down on them from tall downtown buildings.

What she had left behind in Southern California, the sunny skies that belied the seismic threats below, reminded her of a certain kind of patient, the kind who seemed, on the surface, to have it all together. But Chicago's moody weather, its depressed winters, manically overheated summers, its bipolar falls and springs and erratically behaving climate, reminded her of a teenager in torment. And she stayed here, she realized, for the same reason some people ran marathons or climbed mountains: to prove to herself that she could survive.

A snowstorm was brewing in the clouds overhead. Gail didn't like the looks of it, but in her big puffy coat designed for skiing that she had bought from a sporting goods store, she was prepared. She was glad she'd worn it today. Just minutes after she'd arrived at his office, Dr. Lutkin had lured her back out into the blustery weather with the promise of a lunch interview over a Giordano's pizza. She couldn't refuse. Pizza was her weakness.

She was grateful for the oregano-scented warmth of the restaurant. As they waited for their deep dish pizza to come, Dr. Lutkin spoke of the work he did heroically. It was not enough to wait for time to heal his patients' wounds. Change needed to happen now. Sometimes the ways parents knew to help their children weren't helpful at all. And that was where his work, and Gail's, began. That was what his school was good for, restoring a sense of order and structure to their lives. No matter what inner turmoil and confusion the kids endured, their environment would be predictable, reliable, and safe. There was refuge in the routine, which included going to classes just like other kids their age did.

"We've hired the best teachers we could find and we keep the classes small so that our students can get help whenever they need it. I don't want anyone to fall behind in their studies. Our goal is for them to go back to mainstream schools without having to repeat a grade. It's difficult enough for them to deal with the stigma of their diagnoses," Dr. Lutkin told her.

Gail remembered the times she had sat in on the classes they taught at Haven House. Those classes were an afterthought. In fact, they were so basic and remedial that she'd seen kids reading picture books in them. Some of these teenagers had been at the top of their classes before succumbing to mental illness.

"Ensuring that our students get a good education while they're at the school lets them know that we still have faith in their ability to use their minds. Learning about the world around them can help to ease some of their anxieties. The key is having teachers who know how to turn their deficits into strengths."

Dr. Lutkin went on to say that every member of the staff, even the janitors and cooks, played a special role in helping the kids recover. He also believed in working with his patients' families and letting the parents be a part of the solution instead of blaming them for all their children's problems.

Unlike the director of Haven House, Dr. Lutkin had ideas that made a lot of sense to Gail. Sometimes her residency had made her think of famous psychological studies that tested just how far people would go when following orders. Other times she felt like Haven House was a sort of cruel dystopia with an overly complicated system of meaningless rules. She hated having to enforce policies that made no sense to her or the kids. She despised the hospital's rigid system of points and privileges and levels. She didn't see the purpose of all the group therapy sessions where the leaders were so focused on discussing things that had happened inside the hospital that the kids never worked on resolving the problems that had gotten them admitted to it in the first place. No wonder she had lost faith in her chosen specialty.

But it seemed like Dr. Lutkin had thought of everything. Gail liked the idea of working in a place where the treatment was so comprehensive. She just hoped she was up for the challenge.

Janina liked Fridays. Every other weekday at school had the same schedule, but on Fridays, classes ended half an hour early and they had snacks in the lounge before their afternoon activities. And every week, the snacks were different, since the counselors took turns bringing them. Friday snacks could be almost anything, and she liked the surprise. Otherwise, their food choices were totally predictable: mashed potatoes on Mondays, tacos on Tuesdays, lasagna on Wednesdays, turkey burgers on Thursdays. But Fridays were a nice break from the usual pattern. Usually, she used this extra free time to read, write, or draw.

This Friday was special. Not just because Meredith had made Rice Krispies treats, which were the best Janina had ever tasted, but because Devante was here, and because she was hoping he would notice her new hairstyle and like it. She put together a new outfit, too. Her sweater was made of colorful crocheted flowers that were joined together at their petals' edges, and she wore a fitted top underneath it. She had painted the jeans she wore with flowers like the ones in the sweater. And she put her floral sneakers on with it. She sat across from Devante at a little table where they played Scrabble together.

"You made it through your first week!" She smiled at him.

"It feels like so much longer than that," he sighed. "Maybe 'cause I'm getting more sleep now, in between my nightmares."

She felt bad for him. This was the first time he'd told her about that.

"Or maybe it's because you haven't had to go to classes with us yet."

"Is there homework?"

"No. We do everything in class. The only homework we have is to get better."

Devante gave her a skeptical frown. If that was true, then why had Dr. Lutkin given him an assignment during his session today? He had actually used the word "homework" too. Devante was about to say something to Janina about it, but when he looked at her, she seemed to have her mind on other things. The radio had her undivided attention now.

"My name is Tevin. What's yours?" A voice on the radio said.

Janina smiled at the intro to one of her favorite songs.

"I love Tevin Campbell," she sighed. "You know,

if we got married, I wouldn't even have to change my last name. And before you ask, no, the two of us are not related."

"Tevin Campbell? For real?" he laughed. "That's for little girls, yo."

"No it's not." Said Janina.

He could tell from the look on her face that his joke had hurt her feelings. And they took that no teasing rule very seriously around here. He had to come up with something quick.

"Girl, I was just playing. Since this is your jam, let's dance."

She smiled from ear to ear as he took her hand and led her to a part of the lounge where there was enough room to slow dance. He noticed that Nurse Erica was watching them, but all Janina noticed was him. She couldn't believe she was actually holding his hand.

"This is nice. I don't get to dance with boys here. I mean, we don't have dances."

"For real? How long have you been here?"

"Four years. Since I was ten."

"That's a long time."

From across the room, Alejandra eyed the two of them enviously, then turned and looked at Zack.

"Dance with me, Zachary!" Alejandra commanded with a dramatic flourish.

Everyone watched as Alejandra pulled Zack from his seat and led him in an impetuous tango. They looked so funny dancing like that, with Alejandra in her baggy red jeans and Zack in his Nirvana t-shirt. The other kids laughed. The counselors were smiling. Janina felt relieved that they wouldn't get in trouble for this. She was afraid Alejandra might ruin it. But so far, things were okay. And Devante had one hand on her shoulder, and one hand in hers. All of them were having such a good time that they didn't see Janina's parents, even though her mother's lime green blouse and her father's busily patterned sweater made them hard to miss. But the kids didn't hear Janina's parents come in the door. The kids didn't see the shock on their faces when they walked in to find their daughter dancing with a boy. And the kids didn't notice how Janina's parents stood and stared for a long time, growing angrier by the minute.

"Uh-oh. He's about to break it down!" joked Devante.

"I thought you didn't like this song."

"Just because it's played out, that doesn't mean I don't know the words."

And then in unison with Tevin Campbell, Devante and Janina said, "Break ... it ... down..." and laughed.

Janina had never realized just how silly that part of the song sounded until now.

"What kind of music do you like?" she asked Devante.

But before he could answer, her parents were right beside her. Devante froze.

"Janina Brianna Campbell." Her mother said,

quiet-mad.

It was the worst kind of anger, Janina thought. The calm before the storm.

"We were just dancing, Mama." Janina pleaded with her parents. She looked at Devante, who stood there helplessly, then ran to her room. She threw herself on her bed and began to cry.

"You're not here to get a boyfriend."

Her mother's icy voice made her look up from her flowered comforter. There were both of her parents, standing in the doorway.

"But he's not my boyfriend. We're just friends."

"Boys your age are never just friends with girls. They only have one thing on their minds. You hear me?"

"But Mama, Devante's not like that. He's nice."

"If he's so nice, why is he here?"

Her father's words were very painful to hear, and she started crying again.

"Oh, Marvin." Her mother shook her head.

"Janina, honey, I didn't mean—"

"I'm sorry. I'm so sorry." Janina didn't want them to be mad at her.

"It's just that I... that both of us are very disappointed in you."

Her father's words, and the look on his face, cut her like a knife.

"And why were you listening to that worldly music?" her mother asked. "We taught you better than that."

"I know, I know. I'm sorry," Janina sobbed. She wished she could shrink down to the size of an ant and go hide someplace dark where no one would ever find her.

Nurse Erica walked into the midst of the commotion.

"Mr. and Mrs. Campbell, you're really upsetting Janina."

But Janina's father wasn't having it. "She may live at your school, but she's still our daughter and we expect her to live by our rules. She needs discipline. That's one thing she got at her old school that she's not getting here." And then he turned to Janina and reached in his coat pocket. He took out a cassette tape. "Here's something you can listen to. This is from the youth service last Friday night. Wait until you hear the choir."

Janina was still crying, but she took the tape from him.

"Of course, we didn't attend that service, but all the young people really love the new youth pastor." Her mother's little smile did nothing to stop the flow of her tears.

Nurse Erica noticed Janina's distress and told the Campbells, "I think it would be best if you leave now."

"We only came by early so we could beat the snowstorm. We even brought her favorite thing from Harold's." Janina's father held up a bag and smiled. "A quarter dark with mild sauce."

"I'm not hungry," she wept.

Her stomach felt neither upset nor sour. It felt like it didn't exist. Appetite and hunger were meaningless sensations. The sweet, tangy aroma of the mild sauce on the chicken and fries had become irrelevant. She only felt an emptiness inside that didn't want to be filled.

"I'm really sorry to do this, but I must ask both of you to leave." Nurse Erica was firm this time. "Janina is very distressed by this visit."

Both her parents looked hurt and disappointed.

"Alright," Mr. Campbell sighed, then kissed his crying daughter on the forehead. "Love you, sweetie."

Mrs. Campbell kissed her on the cheek. Mr. Campbell put the bag of Harold's chicken on her dresser before he followed his wife out. Janina covered her face with her hands.

"Are you okay?" Nurse Erica asked.

"I'm sorry," Janina said, still crying.

"You have nothing to apologize for."

Just then, a counselor rushed into the room. "Erica, we've got a situation with one of the little kids in the playroom."

"Janina, I have to take care of this. But I'll be back if you need to talk to me, okay?"

"Okay," said Janina as tears streamed down her face. She didn't look up as Nurse Erica and the counselor hurried out.

How could Janina have done this? What was going to happen now? She had disobeyed her parents and her church. She'd been secretly dubbing tapes of the music they didn't want her to listen to for over a year now, and recording songs from the radio. Recording over tapes of church services sometimes! And she already knew how the church felt about dancing. That never stopped her from participating in dance therapy. But this was different. Dancing with a boy when she knew her parents didn't want her to was terrible, and she was a terrible person for doing this.

But they ruined everything!

No, I deserve it.

But they humiliated me in front of everybody!

No, that's what you get.

She was a disappointment.

Children obey your parents in the Lord. Honor thy mother and father. Spare the rod, spoil the child—

She was a terrible daughter. She ought to be punished for what she had done. Severely. She felt so ashamed. How could she ever leave her room again? How could she ever face Devante again? Or should she? Her parents didn't want her to see him again.

They ruined everything!

No, you *ruined everything, crazy girl.*

She needed to talk to someone. She and Dr. Lutkin had made a deal. She had to find him. She stopped crying long enough to go to his office and ask his secretary where he was. But it turned out that he was in meetings for the rest of the day. So she went back in her room.

The girl she saw in the mirror was a girl who

deserved to be punished.

"How could you be so stupid?" she asked herself.

Her eyelids were puffy from crying. She wanted to punch her reflection right between the eyes, but there was no point in trying to smash the shatterproof glass. She couldn't lock herself in her room and, as Alejandra discovered last year, trying to barricade herself in her room would be pointless, too. All the doors opened from the outside. The bathrooms had no doors except the ones on the stalls. But they cleared the floor by enough feet to allow a counselor to crawl underneath if necessary. And sometimes it had been—just not for her. She didn't know why she was thinking about doors just now. Maybe because she wished she could keep people out of her life with them. She thought of something Dr. Lutkin had told her about the doors when she first arrived: "The front door is locked from the outside to protect you, but you are not locked in." The front door was calling to her now. It was the threshold she dreaded most, a portal to punishment and pain.

I deserve to be punished.

She thought again of her parents. She knew why they had come early. It was because of the snow. They had done the same thing last winter. Her father's boss had let the accounting department go home early, and her mother's last clients of the day had canceled their appointments, so the two of them decided to visit her before the roads got bad. She thought of the looks on their faces last winter, so desperate to please her. She thought of the looks on their faces this afternoon, so disappointed in what she had done. She thought of the dress they had just given her for her birthday, a souvenir from a trip she refused to take with them. They had wanted to celebrate their anniversary by bringing her with them to the resort where they had honeymooned in Mexico, but Janina wouldn't go. In a flood of panicked tears she told them no. So they went without her and brought back the pretty cotton dress, embroidered all over with colorful flowers. She opened the door to her wardrobe and looked at the dress hanging on the rod, having just thought of a fitting punishment for herself.

She took off her sweater and jeans and put the dress on. She replaced her boots with a pair of flip-flops. The sandals made a smacking sound as she walked through the lounge past the other kids. She didn't look to see if Devante was still there. Shame on her for thinking about him now. She wasn't supposed to be looking at boys. She wasn't here for that. Shame on her for disobeying her parents. Shame on her for disappointing them. She paused on the landing just before the second floor to take her flip-flops off so that if there were still counselors in the playroom, they wouldn't hear her coming. She turned and looked at the walls that enclosed the stairwell. They were made of glass blocks in many different colors. Such happy colors. She couldn't bear to look at them now. If those walls weren't there, she thought, she could jump right over the railing and fall straight down to the first floor. And if she got hurt, it would serve her right. She bit her lip to stifle her tears and went down the stairs. She was glad she knew her school and its routine well enough to know how to sneak out undetected. By the time she was almost at the first floor, she saw Dr. Lutkin's secretary, Simone, walking from her desk towards the ladies' room. Janina had to seize this moment. No one knew she was in the lobby. No one saw her as she let herself out the front door.

The predatory winter wind blasted her. This was what the old folks at her church called The Hawk. The heavy door thudded closed behind her as cold air penetrated every pore. It stung her all over like thousands of icy cold needles. But she slipped her flip-flops back on and went down the stairs anyway. So what if she was freezing? She deserved it. Condensation wafted before her face every time she exhaled. Her teeth were chattering. She crunched across the salt-covered walkway and into the front lawn, coating her bare toes with a layer of snow so cold it hurt. More snow was starting to fall. She stretched her arms out and opened her hands to catch it. The snowy landscape was all she had now, with the door to her school locked behind her and the gate to the fenced-in yard locked in front of her. Something about the heaviness of the dull grey sky overhead made her start crying again. Her tears felt warm as they streamed down her cheeks. But before she could blink, The Hawk made her tears feel like ice. It wasn't long before her face, hands, and feet were numb.

~~~

Devante felt like Janina's parents were mad at him, too. He left the lounge to go to the bathroom and splash some water on his face, trying to calm his rattled nerves and collect himself, which took longer than he thought it would. When he returned to the lounge he was afraid to go to the girls' wing to talk to Janina, worried her parents might still be there. So he sat down in one of the beanbag chairs and waited for her to return.

"Has anybody seen Janina?" he heard Nurse Erica ask.

The other kids shrugged and shook their heads. Devante got up and ran over to her. "I haven't seen her since her parents came."

He could tell from the nurse's worried expression that things were serious. He didn't think Janina was the type of girl to just disappear like that. And from Nurse Erica's reaction, it looked like she wasn't.

"As soon as you find her, have her come see me. I really don't want her to be alone right now."

Would she try to do something? He had to find her before it was too late.

"She might be in the art room. I'll go see if she's there."

He'd find her. He had to.

CHAPTER 14
EXPOSURE

"And so then the psychiatrist says, 'What, you eat coffee cups for breakfast and only leave the handles? You must be crazy, because the handle is the tastiest part!'"

Gail laughed at Dr. Lutkin's joke as they walked back to the school. She thought their interview had gone well. She had enjoyed the pizza and their conversation. It had been worth venturing back out into the cold. Dr. Lutkin seemed like someone she would like to work for. Then Gail noticed something that looked odd.

"Hey, what's that over by the bushes?"

They stepped off the walkway and walked across the frosty lawn. There was someone crouching in the soft blue shadows of the snow. It was a girl, and she was shivering. The same girl Gail had seen when she came in for her first interview.

"Oh my God!" cried Gail.

The girl wasn't wearing a coat. The short-sleeved dress she wore was far too flimsy for this weather, and so were her shoes. Flip-flops. She might as well be barefoot. What was she doing out here? She could freeze to death!

Dr. Lutkin rushed to Janina's side, took off his coat, and wrapped her in it. He and Gail picked her up and carried her inside.

Once they were safely in the lobby, Dr. Lutkin took hold of Janina's chin and turned her face towards his.

"Janina, can you hear me?"

"Yes," she said, teeth chattering.

Meredith hurried over to them to see what was going on.

As soon as Dr. Lutkin saw her, he said, "Get Erica. Have her meet us in Janina's room."

Devante stood bewildered in the first floor hallway. He couldn't believe he didn't find Janina in the art room. Where could she be? Just then he saw Gail and Dr. Lutkin rush past. They were carrying Janina. What happened? What had she done?

Janina was back in her bed before she knew it. It was all a blur: Dr. Lutkin's coat, Devante's puzzled face in the hallway, the trip upstairs to her third floor room. Now Dr. Lutkin replaced his coat with her blankets. She'd never been so cold in her life. There was someone new in her room, a pretty dark-skinned woman with a head of short natural curls. She said her name was Gail.

"Can you wiggle your fingers and toes?" Gail asked her.

"Yes." She winced.

Her hands and feet were so cold they burned with pain. But she could still move them.

"Good," said Dr. Lutkin. "How long were you outside?"

"I don't know. Not too long. But please, please, please don't tell my parents! I don't want them to know."

If her parents found out she'd done this because of Devante, she'd be in so much trouble with them.

"Alright, alright. Stay calm," Dr. Lutkin told her.

Janina felt like she'd let him down, too. Nurse Erica came in and told Janina to open her mouth, and placed a digital thermometer inside it. Then Gail looked at Janina's hands, feet, and ears. Nurse Erica listened to her heart with a stethoscope. Dr. Lutkin watched from across the room. Janina had never seen him look so worried before. She quickly looked away and stared at the blanket spread across her lap. She didn't want them to feel sorry for her. She didn't want them to know how much her frozen fingers and toes pained her. She didn't want to cry again today. But she almost cried as they examined her. The cold seemed to have settled deep into her bones. It made them ache. Finally, the thermometer beeped and Nurse Erica took it out of her mouth and looked at it.

"It's slightly below normal," Nurse Erica said to Dr. Lutkin. "Janina, you stay in bed and we'll bring you something warm to drink, okay?"

"Okay."

Janina wrapped her blankets more tightly around herself and wondered if she'd ever be warm again. Meanwhile, across the room, Gail was talking to Dr. Lutkin.

"It looks like a very mild case of hypothermia and frostbite," Gail said.

"It's a good thing you both found her when you did," said Nurse Erica on her way out of the room.

Her words made Janina shiver. Dr. Lutkin looked at her, still worried.

"What happened? I thought we had a deal. You promised that you'd come to me or one of the other staff when you felt depressed."

Great. Now he was disappointed in her, too.

"I'm sorry. It was so stupid of me." She tried hard not to cry. "Please promise that you won't tell my parents."

"I won't tell them," said Gail.

"Neither will I. This is just between us. Now please, tell us why you did this."

Janina couldn't even look them in the eye. She looked down at her blanket instead. She couldn't answer them right away. She had to collect herself first. She had to tell her eyes not to cry.

"Okay. My parents don't want me to see Devante anymore. They saw us together, and I got in a lot of trouble for it. I just... I can't... I just can't live like this. Why am I so stupid? Why do I do such stupid things?"

"Don't beat up on yourself."

Dr. Lutkin's words were soft. Janina was glad he didn't yell at her, even though she hadn't kept her promise to him. Maybe she couldn't help it. Maybe it was just a part of her craziness.

She couldn't believe how quickly Nurse Erica came back with a tray of hot chocolate and hot soup and put it on her nightstand. Janina thanked her and then picked up the mug of hot chocolate. It even had marshmallows in it. It was so steaming hot she had to blow on it before she could take her first sip. Dr. Lutkin pulled up a chair beside her bed.

"Now, Janina, because of what happened today, I'm afraid that I will have to put you on restriction until you're feeling better. This is only to keep you safe. You can't have anything that you can harm yourself with. You have to stay in your room, and you can't see any visitors right now. Nurse Erica will stay with you for the rest of the day. Okay?"

"Okay."

Restriction? It had been such a long, long time since they'd put Janina on it. She'd been doing so much better. So much for her plateau. She must be crazier than she thought.

"I wish I had time to do another session with you, but I can't," Dr. Lutkin continued. "But I know you're in good hands with Nurse Erica."

Janina nodded her head sadly. There was

nothing she could do. She had to get well. That's what she was supposed to be here for, right? Eating her soup was a good start. How did Nurse Erica know she liked Chicken & Stars better than regular chicken noodle?

~~~

Gail's mask of professional detachment started slipping as soon as she was in the privacy of Dr. Lutkin's office. All she could think about was Janina shivering in the cold. She could have died! What if they hadn't seen her out there?

"Are you alright?" Dr. Lutkin asked her. "It seems as though this case has brought up a lot of emotion for you."

The first time she was here, he was behind his desk, and she sat in a chair that faced it. But now they were in another area of his office, sitting in two plum colored armchairs near the toys. This must be where he saw his patients. She'd promised herself she wouldn't talk about her reason for wanting to become a psychiatrist, at least not during interviews. She had been afraid she'd become too emotional. She'd never told anyone about it before, but for the first time since finishing medical school, she felt like she was dealing with someone she could expose her vulnerability to, and so she told him her story.

"My brother had his first psychotic episode when he was sixteen." She began as though she was presenting a case history of someone else's brother, but it didn't make it easier to tell. "I was in my first year of medical school and had come back home to L.A. for a visit. Shawn was completely incoherent and behaving erratically. He was suffering from Cotard's delusion and told me he was dead. I was so afraid for him. I wanted to do whatever I could to help him. He needed to get to a hospital, but I was worried I couldn't drive us there safely with him being so agitated.

"So I called 911. Somehow—even though I told them it was a medical emergency—they ended up sending a police car instead of an ambulance, and the officers were really rough with him. They charged him with resisting arrest. I begged them to let him see a doctor, but they wouldn't listen. They took him to jail. While he was in there, before I could reach our parents about posting bail for him, he hanged himself in his cell. He left a note. It said, 'I'm already dead.'"

Even now, Gail couldn't think of that note without shaking. Dr. Lutkin put a hand on her shoulder, as if to steady her.

"I'm so sorry for your brother. Such a terrible loss. It sounds like the police really mishandled the situation. Did your family ever get any justice?"

"No, we never did. It happened a couple years before the Rodney King beating, and the LAPD was above the law back then. It was only after a year of therapy that I finally stopped blaming myself for what happened. I had to take a leave of absence from med school during that time. When I came back, I changed my specialty from radiology to psychiatry. Since I wasn't able to help Shawn, I wanted to help other kids so what happened to my brother wouldn't happen to them."

Once she had learned that what Shawn probably had, schizophrenia, was the most under-researched disease in the world, Gail felt as though she'd found her calling in life. She had come back to medical school with a new sense of purpose. Everything she did after she returned was in her brother's memory.

Dr. Lutkin sighed and leaned forward in his chair. "I also had a brother who suffered from mental illness as a boy. And with the way that institutions were back in the 50s, he was subjected to so many brutal treatments. He's the reason I became a psychiatrist."

Gail thought he sounded just as nervous and reluctant as she did when she told him about Shawn. From the tone of his voice, he sounded like it was his first time telling anyone.

"I think that both our brothers would have recovered here," Gail told him.

She noticed how carefully selected and high-quality the toys on this side of the office were, neatly lined up on a wide row of built-in shelves. There were costumes hanging on a child-sized coat rack and a few props, like a magic wand. A medieval-style tapestry hung on the adjoining wall. The tapestry featured a knight and a fair-haired maiden, and went well with the collection of toy shields on the top shelf.

"Absolutely. Treating suicidal patients is very difficult work, especially when they're so young. They have so much to live for, though that's the last thing they want to hear. But knowing that they do have so much to live for and have so much ahead of them is what makes working with them worthwhile. Still, it takes a lot out of you, which is why we have weekly debriefing meetings for the staff. After all, how can we be sensitive to patients' emotional needs if our own are not taken into account?"

"It's only been a few weeks since I've worked with patients and today is a reminder of just how overwhelming it can be," Gail replied.

She wished she hadn't used the word "overwhelming" just now. She didn't want him to think she couldn't handle it.

"You did a tremendous job," said Dr. Lutkin, much to her surprised relief. "I was already planning to offer you a position after our conversation over lunch today, but now I've got something else in mind. I'd like for you to have more responsibilities than the other counselors. You could help me facilitate the parent support group meetings on Saturdays. I also would like to supervise you as you work with a few patients individually. What would you think of that?"

She thought it was a dream come true.

"That sounds great. It actually sounds a lot like a residency."

"It's a shame our school isn't large enough to offer a formal residency program, because if it was, I'd steal you away from Dr. Hoffman." His eyes twinkled with mischief. Then he looked at his watch. "Sorry to cut this discussion short, but I have another meeting soon. I'll see you tomorrow morning at the parent support group."

Gail agreed to meet him the next day, feeling calmer than she'd felt in months. So this was where she'd be working now. She'd finally found the right place.

CHAPTER 15
QUARANTINE

Nurse Erica was going through all of Janina's things. She opened all her dresser drawers and took out anything with a cord and anything that was sharp or that could be broken into sharp pieces. She took Janina's mirror, her pens and pencils, her pencil sharpener, her boombox, and even her bras and put them all into a box. All Janina could do was watch from her bed. She had buried herself up to her neck in her covers. Even after having the hot chocolate and soup, she still felt like she'd never get warm. Soon they'd take the box away, just as they'd taken the chicken away. But that was only because she'd asked them to put it in the refrigerator and save it for later. She was still too upset to eat very much.

"You'll get everything back soon," Nurse Erica reassured her.

Next she went through Janina's art supplies. Janina wondered what else would end up in the box.

Nurse Erica took out a pack of felt-tipped markers.

"You can keep these. I know you like to write."

Janina felt relieved. Nurse Erica was thorough, but fair. She picked up Janina's black sketchbook.

"Don't worry, I'm not going to read your diary. I just have to flip through to make sure there isn't anything sharp in here, okay?"

"Okay."

But Janina wasn't worried since it wasn't her diary. She didn't mind if Nurse Erica saw it. After all, she'd written it for other people to read. As the nurse looked through it, she smiled.

"Did you draw all these pictures?"

"Yeah. It's my graphic novel. You can read it if you want to. I don't mind."

"Really?"

Janina couldn't believe Nurse Erica was so excited about reading it.

"Sure," Janina said, smiling for the first time since she'd come in from the cold.

"How do you pronounce the title?"

"It's pronounced just like 'syndrome.' And it's about kids who are mental patients but also have psychic superpowers."

Just then someone knocked on the door. Nurse Erica tucked the box of contraband under her arm and went to see who it was. From her bed, Janina saw it was Devante. Even though she was glad he came to check on her, she didn't feel like smiling anymore. Nurse Erica stepped out into the hallway to talk to him.

"Sorry, I can't let you see her right now," she told him.

"Is she okay?"

"Yes, she's doing much better. I have to get back in there."

Nurse Erica went back in and closed the door softly behind her, leaving Devante standing there by himself. He didn't understand why he couldn't see her if she was doing so much better. And why was Nurse Erica holding that cardboard box? Was Janina packing? Was she about to leave? He turned and looked through the windowed door to the lounge, and noticed Ed watching him. He went back to the lounge since there was no point in waiting in the girls' wing.

"They won't let you see her, huh?" said Ed as Devante walked past.

"No."

"She's being quarantined," Ed explained. "Had she been coughing, sneezing, throwing up, anything like that?"

"No, she wasn't sick. I just saw her, like, an hour ago."

Now he was really confused. Why would they quarantine her if she wasn't sick?

"Sorry, but that means she must have tried to off herself. Lutkin thinks teen suicide is contagious, so he quarantined her."

Suicide? So she really was just like all those other kids in the mood disorders group? But why?

Were things really that bad with her parents? As unbelievable as Ed's explanation had been, he looked like he knew what he was talking about. Ed looked like he knew about contagious things, anyway. He always wore rubber gloves. One time, Devante even saw him wearing a paper mask like a surgeon.

"I think you're supposed to be in anxiety disorders group with us, aren't you?"

"I guess," Devante shrugged. He had forgotten all about that.

"Better get over there now so we won't be late," Ed said nervously.

Dr. Lutkin had explained that Devante's stress disorder was an anxiety disorder, and that witnessing what had happened to Monica was what caused it. Devante was surprised to see how many other kids had anxiety problems, too. The two therapists who led the group told Devante they wouldn't make him go first or last, but encouraged him to say something before the session was over. They let Ed start.

"I know everybody keeps saying to just take the gloves off, but I can't do that yet. I think I'll just try one glove. I'm gonna see what it's like to go a whole week without wearing a glove on my left hand."

Ed took off his left glove and everyone clapped for him.

"If my left hand is still okay by next Friday, then maybe I can take off my right glove, too."

"That must have been a really hard choice for you to make, Ed," said one of the therapists. "What led you to do it?"

"I'm so tired of being afraid. I'm so worried about so many things, and I'm so afraid of being afraid that just worrying about it gives me panic attacks sometimes, you know?"

Devante and the other kids in the group all nodded. He was glad he wasn't the only one who felt that way. But he wasn't going to tell them about what he was afraid of. When he explained that to Jonathan, one of the therapists leading the group, he encouraged him to share something else.

"I guess I can tell you why I'm here. It's because of stress. I lot of things happened all at once. My parents got divorced, we moved to a different neighborhood, I started high school, and then..."

He couldn't tell them about Monica. Not yet.

"I can't talk about the rest of it right now. But it got so bad that I tried to kill myself."

It was so strange to finally say those words. But he knew he wasn't the only one there who had tried the same thing. A few of the kids in this group were also in the mood disorders group with him. They all had their reasons. But what about Janina? Why had she done it? The whole time he had known her, though it wasn't that long, she seemed like she was pretty stable. She was definitely more stable than he was. What did that mean? He wished he could talk to her and get some answers. He needed to understand.

When the session was over, it was time for dinner. The afternoon seemed so much longer without

Janina around. At least he had Ed to talk to. He noticed that a few of the kids in their group didn't join them for dinner. Instead, they put their coats on and went to the lobby to wait for their parents to pick them up.

"They're transitional," Ed explained. "They get to go home after group."

Going home was hard to even think of right now. He wasn't sure when he'd ever be ready. How long would it take? He still couldn't sleep at night.

"I need to go check on something before I can eat. You can come with me if you want," said Ed.

"Okay." Devante shrugged.

He followed Ed across the cafeteria to the kitchen, where the cooks seemed to be expecting him. They even gave him a hairnet to wear. Ed walked solemnly across the kitchen, carefully looking at every pot and pan and tray of food. Then they opened the refrigerator so he could look inside.

"I have to check the expiration dates," Ed explained.

Devante saw Janina's name written on a paper bag from Harold's Chicken. His heart sank.

"Haven't seen you around before. You new?" One of the cooks asked him.

"Yeah," he said.

"Well, if there's ever anything you need, you just let me know."

"Thanks." Devante smiled faintly.

Ed was finishing up his inspection. He seemed satisfied. "Good, good." He nodded and left the kitchen.

"Why'd you go back there?" Devante asked once they sat down at a table.

"They let me check on things and make sure it's clean. The counselors already know that's the only way I can eat most days. You can never be too careful, you know."

Ed took a fork and held it up, examining it closely for spots that the dishwasher might have missed.

"Yeah, I know," said Devante.

He didn't feel much like eating. He wished he'd been more careful this afternoon. If only he'd been paying attention. If only he'd seen Janina's parents coming. If only he'd been there when she came back through the lounge. Maybe he could have stopped her. But once again, he'd been in the wrong place at the wrong time. He felt so useless.

When they finished eating, Devante asked Ed if he wanted to play Nintendo, and Ed agreed. So Devante picked up a controller and handed it to Ed, who took it in his gloved right hand. And then he realized he wouldn't be able to play with just one hand. He would need both hands, not just the one that was protected by a rubber glove. He panicked, and reached into his pocket to retrieve his left glove.

"Wait, man. You don't have to do it," Devante said once he realized what Ed was doing.

"Do you have any idea how many germs could be living on that thing right now?" Ed pleaded. "Do you know how many people have touched it without washing their hands?"

"You can wash your hands afterwards." Devante thought it sounded like a decent compromise. But Ed shook his head.

"No. It's not good enough. I need more protection."

Devante was disappointed to see Ed put the glove back on. It was a gesture of defeat. It reminded him of his flashback the other day, and of the nightmares that had been keeping him awake ever since the one decent night of sleep he'd gotten after weeks of sleeplessness.

"Sorry," said Ed, noting his new friend's disappointment, "but I can't do it. It's just too hard. There's just something about Fridays. They're so uneven. They break the pattern. The schedule bothers me."

They started playing Dr. Mario. Devante liked it because it was a falling shapes puzzle like Tetris, with pills falling into a bottle of dancing viruses.

Without ever taking his eyes off the screen, Ed said, "You know how I ended up here? One day my friend invited me over to make robots with his Lego Technics set. He'd just gotten over strep throat. I think he could've gotten his germs all over the bricks, because a few days later, I came down with it. I was never so sick in my life. My throat swelled up so much that I couldn't swallow, and after a while I couldn't breathe, either. I had to go to Children's Memorial Hospital for a few days. All my doctors and nurses were wearing masks. I asked why, and they said they had to since I was contagious. They even let me have one. One of the nurses was nice enough to let me have some gloves, too. After I got home, I wanted to keep wearing them. I wanted to wear them to school, but my parents wouldn't let me. It was so bad I couldn't go to school without them, and I couldn't eat in restaurants. My parents couldn't take it anymore, so they brought me here."

"You can always try again tomorrow. Taking off the glove, I mean," said Devante.

Suddenly he realized Ed was getting the upper hand. Ed was vaporizing the dancing viruses in his bottle with pill after pill after pill, while Devante was in danger of losing Dr. Mario's war against germs.

CHAPTER 16
INTENTION AND ACTION

Trying so hard not to cry again. Promised myself I wouldn't. Hearing the voices of my old classmates in my head taunting me, "Crybaby cry, crybaby cry," over & over & over again. And when they said that, it only made me cry harder.

Don't cry. Don't.

I'll let the sky cry for me instead. The snow can be my frozen tears.

Today is the worst day of my life so far. Even worse than everything that happened at my old school. Even worse than sixth grade! My parents humiliated me in front of everybody, they don't want me to see Devante anymore, and now I'm on restriction. I do such stupid things, and that's why I deserve to suffer. I should just freeze to death. I could have today. Everyone says it's a good thing they found me when they did, or I would have. But I don't care. I'm so stupid and useless and worthless anyway.

Dr. Lutkin said he's not going to tell my parents what happened. What if he only said that to make me calm down? What if he didn't really mean it? I mean, so far he's always done what he said he'd do, but what if this time it's only a trick? What if he's just telling me what he thinks I want to hear so I won't go any crazier? Today I feel like I broke my mind & I don't know how to fix it. I'm such a mess and I can't do anything right. And that's why they put me on restriction. And that's why I have to write in here with a marker. They took away so many things, even my bras! Oh no, what if Devante saw them? Nurse Erica took the box of the things I couldn't have with her when she opened the door for him when he came by earlier, and I think they might have been at the top of the pile. How can you kill yourself with a bra anyway? That's what I'd like to know. Not like anyone would tell me. Actually, that was only a rhetorical question. It's hard to think of this place as a school when you get put on suicide watch.

I just really, really hope nobody tells my parents.

I'm in enough trouble with them as it is. Why did they have to come so early?

Janina put her marker in her notebook and closed it. She couldn't bring herself to write what she was really thinking. Journaling always helped her sort out her feelings, but there were certain feelings and thoughts she couldn't put on paper. She knew she had good parents. She'd been here long enough to know how fortunate she was. Plenty of kids were here because of their parents. The counselors had taught all of them about emotional and verbal abuse. She had showered and dressed every morning with girls who bore scars that weren't all from self-inflicted wounds. Her parents would never do that.

"How are you feeling?" asked Nurse Erica. She was still sitting in the room reading Janina's graphic novel.

"I finally feel warm," said Janina. Once her arms had warmed up and her fingers stopped hurting, she'd been able to take the blanket off her shoulders and write.

"Good. I'm just going to take your temperature one more time, okay? I didn't want to interrupt you while you were writing."

One of the things Janina liked about Nurse Erica was that she always told you what she was going to do before she did it. She didn't just sneak up on people and force medication or shots on them.

The thermometer beeped. Her temperature was back to normal again, but her emotions remained in a knot that she couldn't untangle. How did today go from being one of the best days of her life to one of the worst? Her mood was smudged by sadness, her emotions smeared downwards from happiness to despair. She had soared so high and fallen so far. The speed with which her spirit plummeted was frightening. She wondered if this was what Alejandra felt like. She wished her emotions could be as numb as her fingers and toes had been. How fragile the feeling of happiness had been, so easily shattered by her parents' clumsy intrusion. But how could she get mad at them? They were good parents. And she was the one who had disobeyed. Now look what she'd done. She'd ruined her afternoon, and Nurse Erica's too. Now both of them were stuck in her room for who knew how long. Sure, she deserved to be punished, but why did her nurse have to suffer, too?

"I'm sorry."

Nurse Erica looked up from Janina's sketchbook. "I told you before, you have nothing to apologize for."

"What do you mean? It's my fault you're stuck here with me. I should have just done what my parents wanted."

"But what about what you wanted?"

"It doesn't matter what I want."

"Why not?"

"Because I'm crazy and not capable of making rational decisions. Because I can't do anything right. Because I didn't turn out the way they wanted me to." Without even realizing it, Janina had made both her hands into tight, angry fists. "Sorry, I shouldn't have said that about them."

"You know, sometimes when you get really angry about something and you don't express your anger, you can turn it inward against yourself. Seems to me like you might be angry at them."

Janina was surprised to hear the words out loud. Angry? At her parents? What right did she have to be mad at them? But she was.

~~~

Dear Shawn,

Today I had a chance to save a girl's life. I've been in life-or-death situations before, but nothing like this. Never before have I found myself standing between the intention to commit suicide and the act itself. I found the girl, Janina, shivering in the snow, trying to freeze herself to death.

I was coming back from an interview with Dr. Lutkin over a late lunch at a Chicago-style pizza place. If we had ordered dessert, if we had chosen to go back into the school through a side door, if we had gotten stuck in traffic, if I hadn't happened to look down at the ground, Janina could have been lost. Finding her like that was another reminder of just how fragile life is, and just how vulnerable we all are.

I don't know why she did it. I don't know anything about her yet. But something must have happened. Something must be very wrong for her to have gone from her warm little room full of artwork she made herself, out into the freezing cold in summer clothes. I hope she will be all right. We found her in time. That makes all the difference.

I know it doesn't make up for what happened to you. I still feel bad about it. That's why I keep writing to you, even though you're gone. There is so much I wish I could have told you, and so many interesting things I never got the chance to explain. You always had so many questions. I like to imagine what you would be asking me about if you were still here to ask me. Writing these letters to you is a way of keeping your memory alive.

I find myself thinking strange thoughts sometimes when I remember you. Today I thought about how you never had a chance to see snow. I wonder what you would have thought about it. I wonder if you would have liked it.

I don't think I will ever stop wishing that I could have stopped you or that I could have gotten you the help you needed. You would like The Harrison School so much, Shawn. It looks so pretty in the snow. It's like a little castle in a snow globe. It's a nice place. They could have helped you there. They could have helped you if you let them. But would you have let them? Or would you have gone out into the snow to freeze?

The man in the sharkskin suit smiled smugly.

"Rebecca took me on a tour the other day. This really is quite a place," he said to Dr. Lutkin.

His name was Peter Roark, and he was an executive from PHEA. He had come back with Rebecca to meet with Dr. Lutkin in his office.

"Thank you," said Dr. Lutkin, doubting Peter's sincerity.

Dr. Lutkin was so tired of having to deal with PHEA. Working with them wasn't his idea. He had been hoping another alternative would eventually present itself, but so far it hadn't. And so, for the past five years, he had been stuck with them, having these dreadful meetings with an ever-changing cast of characters since PHEA was constantly hiring and firing new executives. He had hoped in vain that they might find some harmonious way to work together. He had turned a blind eye to so many things they had done that had displeased him. But he had a feeling that this time things would be different, and that he would have to do things differently.

"Dr. Lutkin, I'm going to get right to the point," said Rebecca. "PharmaCo does not want to continue working with you. This will be your last clinical trial."

There was as much certainty and finality in her words as in her actions at the restaurant. Dr. Lutkin thought of how she had crossed off her half salad with her utensils and hidden its remains beneath her napkin, dismissing it. Out of sight, out of mind. He was not about to have The Harrison School disposed of in the same manner.

"Surely there must be some other pharmaceutical companies looking for a control group. What about Cabot or Riser?" Dr. Lutkin asked.

"I personally pursued that option, but neither of them are interested, nor are any of the other larger drug companies. They don't like the way your results compare to theirs. What can I say? You make them look bad," Peter sneered.

"It seems absurd that we should be penalized by PharmaCo because denoxamine doesn't work, but psychotherapy does. I see what they're doing. Their idea of a control group is a bunch of patients going through withdrawal and all its horrific side effects. And somehow this passes for science!" Dr. Lutkin tried to contain his outrage.

"As interesting as it would be to have a discussion about science and philosophy with you, we really need to get down to business. In six months, this facility will lose its only lifeline. Rebecca has already told you your two choices: make this place into a traditional mental hospital or raise your tuition."

"That is not at all what Dr. Olmsted and I envisioned when we started this school sixteen years ago. It was to be a place of healing, not of punishment. Not another Haven House." Dr. Lutkin shook his head.

"Well what did you expect?" snapped Rebecca. "PHEA stands for Psychiatric *Hospital* Enterprises of America. We are in the hospital business. And insurance isn't going to pay for all your little frills and fringe benefits and warm, fuzzy feelings. We don't run day spas. We run hospitals!"

"Yes. You run hospitals right into the ground. And I won't let you do that here."

He realized now that all this time he had been doing a disservice to the patients he cared so much about by sticking his head in the sand. He felt like a hypocrite for insisting that they confront their problems while he had spent all his time avoiding confrontation with PHEA. But this time was different. This time he would have to fight.

"You might be the king of your little castle, but you're really nothing but a figurehead. What are you going to do, Dr. Lutkin?" Not giving him a chance to reply, Peter snidely added, "If that's even your real name."

Stunned, Rebecca stared at him, and then at Dr. Lutkin.

"What are you talking about?" she asked.

"I had a private detective do a little research on you, sir." Peter locked eyes with Dr. Lutkin and didn't look away. "And it seems that you sprang to life at the ripe old age of seventeen. There are no records of you ever going to junior high or high school, the Boy Scouts or Little League. Everything starts in 1957, when you got your baptismal record from a Greenwich Village priest who's since been excommunicated for his ties to organized crime. Apparently he was in charge of the underworld's equivalent of the federal witness protection program. He helped fugitives change their names and disappear."

"I don't know what you're talking about," said Dr. Lutkin, fumbling with some papers on his desk.

"Sure you don't. Regardless, we would be willing to overlook all of that. Who are we to judge? We're no angels in this industry. We'll let you keep your job. Your medical credentials are legitimate, and that's all that truly matters to us. Two choices, Dr. Lutkin. That's all you get. Now which will it be?"

Two choices, and both of them traps. Two choices, both of which would leave his patients stranded, lessen the quality of their care, and rob them of experiences that were crucial to the healing process. Two choices were being given to him by two people who had no respect for the work he was trying to do or the importance of it. Two choices governed only by the need for profits. Nothing was further from what the school was intended for. If these were the only choices he had, if this was all that PHEA could do for him, he was better off without them.

"I'm taking a third option." Peter and Rebecca looked stunned. "I'm going to buy this school back from you."

Janina lay on the front stairs. Devante picked her up. Her body was a cold, dead weight in his arms. Her limbs were as limp as the stems of wilted flowers. He held her close to him. He tried not to cry, but couldn't stop his tears from falling into her hair. He looked at her face again, and realized he was holding Monica, not Janina. Why was this happening again? He screamed and screamed, and the sound of his own voice woke him up.

There was light coming from outside. He could see the hallway through the window in his door. He got up and went out into the hall, where he found Carlos headed toward his room.

"Another bad dream, huh?" Carlos asked.

"Yeah."

"You want me to get you something to help you go back to sleep?"

"Nah. I don't think I want to sleep again for a

really long time."

"Want to talk about it?"

Devante considered it. "Nah."

"As long as you're up, we could go over to the lounge. You can help me stay awake while I study."

So Devante walked with Carlos through the doors to the lounge. There were psychology textbooks on one of the tables. *Homework never ends, does it?* Devante thought as he watched Carlos take out a notebook and pen.

"You're still in school?"

"Yup. I used to be a pharmacist, but now I'm getting my Master's Degree in counseling psychology."

Devante sat on the couch.

"It sure is quiet. Am I the only one with nightmares or does everybody else just take sleeping pills?"

Carlos looked up from his books. "Some of them do. Others find that writing in a journal helps. Or talking about their nightmares."

"I don't think I could talk about it." Devante shook his head.

"Why not?"

"I don't know. I guess I'm scared to talk about it. If I talk about it, I might start feeling like it's happening all over again, and I don't know if I can take that. I'm trying so hard to forget."

"What are you afraid will happen if you remember?"

"That I'll go crazy again. That I'll be so crazy I

won't even be able to talk to people anymore, like I was before. But you know something? In group today, Ed said that sometimes the fear of his own panic attacks is really what makes him panic."

"Sounds like you can relate to that."

"Yeah, I really can." Devante realized he was sitting on the same couch where, a few hours earlier, Ed had decided to put his glove back on. He got up and started pacing. "It's so overwhelming to feel anything. I wish I could just be numb all the time. I'm afraid that if I talk about it, I won't be able to stop feeling scared and depressed and angry. I wish I could sleep. I couldn't sleep at all when I was at home. Then when I got here, I could sleep again but I have nightmares, like, all the time. Do you really think if I talk about it, the nightmares will go away?"

"Honestly, I think it's not that simple. But that's the first step. You're right, you probably *will* feel a huge flood of emotions when you finally talk about what happened. And there are other ways you can express what's going on in your mind without using any words. That's why we have art therapy, drama therapy, even music therapy."

"I haven't played the piano since it happened."

"Why don't you give it a try?"

"Maybe I will in the morning." Devante yawned. Maybe all that pacing had tired him out. "I'm starting to feel tired again. But I think I'll take a sleeping pill just in case."

Carlos met him back in his room and gave him

the medicine. Devante lay in bed and waited for it to take effect. Great waves of drowsiness swept over him, then finally pulled him under. On this pill, falling asleep meant falling into an abyss. Sleep was what the medication anchored him to, and he couldn't escape it. He couldn't wake up from his dreams, no matter how bad they got. All he could do was stand by helplessly as everyone around him—Monica, Janina, Grandma, his parents, his brother, and even Carlos and Dr. Lutkin—were killed right in front of him. Over and over again authority figures, from the toy cops at the police academy, to the real cops, to President Clinton, shook their heads and said, "You were in the wrong place at the wrong time." The bullets were meant for Devante, but they always missed. The pill had sentenced him to sleep, condemned him to facing the same horrific images for six hours. He was relieved to finally wake up and tell himself that every horror he had witnessed was only part of a series of bad dreams. The whole experience left him feeling more awake than he'd felt in weeks, yet completely unnerved.

He thought of what Carlos had told him last night. Would music help him? He went to the music room Janina had showed him and sat at the piano. The feeling of his fingertips on ivory keys was familiar and unfamiliar at the same time. Before, it had meant one thing, but now it meant something else. Playing the piano would never be the same again. He looked up and noticed the wallpaper border around the ceiling, which was a pattern of musical notes. Curious, he played them. Just as he suspected, they were just scales, the kind of thing he'd warm up with. The kind of thing he had had to convince Monica to warm up with.

"What do I need to do that for?" she'd laugh.

"I already know you're a good *singer*," he'd tell her. "But I want to help you become a good *musician*."

Her voice was like honey. Her voice was the color of dusk. The scales were the musical stairs she'd climb up and down to exercise it. After a while she'd tell him it was like warming up for a track meet. He played and she sang and all those years of playing piano to drown out the sound of his parents fighting downstairs (back at the old house, which was so big that he and his brother had a sitting room with a piano right outside their bedrooms) paid off. Devante played and Monica sang and Grandma said he played like his grandfather and Monica sang like Lena Horne. Devante played and Monica sang and the big piano finally seemed at home in Grandma's front room behind the window with the big blue and white "Warning: We Call Police" sign in it.

Music was pouring out of him now. He was playing with feeling, not just with his fingers, not just from muscle memory, but from pain. The somber notes of "Moonlight Sonata" gave way to the grief of Mozart's "Lacrimosa" and he could not stop himself or the memories that playing brought up for him.

Monica had joked that it was her piano. She had eyed it with envious wonder on that late summer day the movers brought it off the truck. She had watched its journey up Grandma's stairs and into the house from her yard next door. The piano, and the music that Devante and Monica had made with it, had brought them closer together. As she taught him how to navigate the distance between their neighborhood and the magnet school they went to, he taught her how to navigate sheet music. And the time they spent playing and singing together was rewarded when they secured a place for themselves in the school spring talent show. Their time together had also made Devante realize he liked Monica as more than just a friend.

He wanted to surprise her on Valentine's Day. Instead of giving her gifts at school, he waited until that night to go to her house with a red rose and a teddy bear so he could ask her to be his girlfriend. But he never got to ask her anything. It was all his fault, having his back turned to the street, wearing the same hat and jacket as a boy in trouble with a rival gang...

"She took the bullets for you," said the paramedics.

"You were in the wrong place at the wrong time," the cops had told him.

How could a miracle and a tragedy happen side by side, in the same split second? Why her and not him? Why play without her singing?

It was the most beautiful music Janina had ever heard, and also the saddest. It was like he was saying something that couldn't be put in words. After her early morning "house call" with Dr. Lutkin, she was freed from the constraints of restriction and told that she was allowed to leave her room again. She was late for breakfast because the counselors wouldn't let her go downstairs until she put some other layers on with her sundress. She had seen Devante leaving the cafeteria just as she got there, and once she finished her breakfast (the leftover chicken from yesterday), she followed the sound of his music. Not wanting to interrupt, she stood in the doorway and listened. She didn't want to tell him how much she enjoyed his playing until he stopped.

"That was really good."

When he turned around to look at her, there was a coldness in his eyes she'd never seen before. He looked like a stranger.

"How could you do that to me, Monica?" he yelled at her.

Frightened and confused, she asked, "Who's Monica?"

Devante realized what he'd just said: her name, out loud, for the first time since it happened. And then he realized who he'd said it to.

"She's dead. Monica's dead. And you were gonna kill yourself, too!"

Janina couldn't believe how angry he was. She tried to calm him down by saying, "But I'm better now."

Devante couldn't believe she could talk about what she'd done that way, shrugging it off like it was the same as getting over a cold.

"How could you do that to yourself? How could you do that to me? I never want to talk to you or see you again!"

How could he say that to her? He didn't even know what happened. She couldn't let this go. She had to say something. And so, for the first time, she found the right words to say in her own defense, and said them.

"I did that because of my parents, Devante. Not because of you! Besides, you wanted to erase yourself, remember? So it's not fair to get mad at me for my suicidal tendencies when you've got the exact same thing!"

"I had a good reason to want to die. I'm still trying to figure out if my life's worth living."

"Aren't we all? You, me, everyone in our mood disorders group, everyone at this school, maybe even our therapists and counselors and our parents! Yesterday I thought maybe I had found something that really made me happy about my life until my parents showed up and ruined everything. And then I talked to Nurse Erica and she helped me see that I got mad at myself when really I was mad at them."

"Are you still mad at yourself?" Devante was a little calmer now.

"No," she said softly. "Now I'm mad at my parents. And I'm mad at you."

She couldn't believe how easy it was for her to admit it.

"Why are you mad at me?" He looked as

surprised as she'd felt.

"'Cause you were going to stop being friends with me."

"We can still be friends. You just have to promise me that you'll never try to kill yourself again, okay?"

And just then she realized how much she meant to him.

"Okay, as long as you promise me the same thing."

Janina stepped closer to the piano and reached out to Devante, who stood up and shook her hand without ever letting his eyes leave hers.

CHAPTER 19

BRINGING UP PARENTS

Running a support group meeting was something Gail felt somewhat qualified to do. Back home in California after Shawn died, she had been in one herself as she dealt with her grief. After six months of meetings she was getting things sorted out, had shed the pounds she'd gained when overeating was her only source of comfort, had reclaimed a place for herself in her Chicago medical school, and was tapering off her antidepressant prescription. That's when the group leader had come to her with a question.

"Have you ever thought about becoming a psychiatrist?" he asked. "You've been great with the other people in the group. I think you have a lot to offer."

The question had come at the perfect time, as Gail had been considering it. Being told that she had a lot to offer was the confirmation she needed. It seemed fitting to have this opportunity, though the setting was drastically different. She had traded palm trees for snow and a church annex for a school gymnasium that had once been a glamorous hotel ballroom.

"How's Janina doing?" Gail asked Dr. Lutkin as soon as she saw him in the gym.

"She's improved significantly since yesterday," he said as he gave Gail two folding chairs to add to the circle in the center of the gym. "I saw her this morning."

Gail was relieved. She'd been worried about her. Soon, with the help of some counselors, they had everything set up for the parent support group, a circle of chairs in the middle of the room and a table of snacks for later. Before long the parents started to arrive. The snow hadn't stopped them. Their faces were lined with anguish. Their sorrows united them. After they took their seats, Dr. Lutkin introduced Gail to the group. He'd called her Dr. Thomas, but she encouraged them to call her by her first name. And then it was time for the new parents to introduce themselves. Ms. Lewis and Mr. Monroe, Devante's mother and father, went first.

"I didn't know what kinds of problems my son was having," Ms. Lewis said. "After the shooting, I threw myself into activism so I wouldn't have to deal with my own grief. I want to build a community center and name it after Monica, in her memory. But since I was so busy with that, I was never home.

"I found out later that Devante couldn't sleep. He would play video games all night with the sound turned off. And he wasn't eating, either. He lost so much weight, and I didn't even realize it. I mean, the kids wear their clothes so baggy these days, but still, I should have noticed. He missed two whole weeks of school and I didn't even know! He was hiding in the basement while I was gone and his grandmother was watching TV or out on errands with me.

"His school called about him missing so many classes. So the next day I drove him there myself. I knew something was wrong when I dropped him off that morning. And then the police called and told me he tried to jump off a bridge over the expressway..."

By now she was in tears. Much to her surprise, Mr. Monroe compassionately took her hand to comfort her. Then Mr. Monroe spoke.

"I can't let Justine take all the blame for what happened to our son. I should have been more understanding. I should have listened more. Instead I was trying to make him into someone he's not, and I belittled him for his taste in music and clothes. And even..." He paused as his voice wavered, stopped as he began to cry, then started again. "...even his choice of girlfriend. All I ever thought about was how what he did reflected on me. It seems so selfish now. We almost lost our son forever."

Mr. Monroe went on to tell them that it hadn't been easy finding out about this school. He said that when he got the phone call about his son's suicide attempt, he rushed to the hospital where Devante was being held for the 72 hours in a room that looked like a prison cell. Then he rushed back to his office, not to work, but to ask a coworker a rather difficult question regarding a confidence that she had once shared about her own troubled son. And the answer was this place.

Gail could tell that the other parents were deeply moved by their story. Many of them had been through the same thing. Another mother turned to Ms. Lewis and Mr. Monroe. Gail thought she looked like she felt terribly guilty.

"My husband and I can relate to what both of you are going through," she said, allowing a tear to stream down her cheek and fall to the collar of the color-blocked suit jacket she was wearing. "We always wanted a family. I got pregnant so many times, but Janina was the only one who made it. She was our miracle baby. When she was only ten years old, I walked in on her one day with a... you know those metal compasses they use to draw circles, with the sharp point at the end? Well Janina was sitting on her floor, stabbing one of her self-portraits with it. She even wrote a note. All it said was, 'I am stupid. I am no good' over and over again. And that was when we knew we had to bring her here."

Mr. Campbell took his wife's hand and squeezed it.

"Her school counselor told us we should watch for signs," he said.

So these were Janina's parents. Gail got Dr. Lutkin's attention after one of the other parents started talking. She took him aside.

"Are you sure we shouldn't tell them about what happened yesterday?" she whispered.

"Believe me, if it had been any other patient, I would never have agreed to this. But after working so hard to get her to open up to us, I don't want to risk losing her trust. All her life she has experienced adults as intrusive and controlling. If I tell her parents about yesterday, that's how she'll see me."

And then they returned to the sad group of parents. Gail tried to be fully present as she led the discussion and listened to what they had to say, but found herself thinking of Janina and wishing she knew more about her case.

∿∿

Janina had hurried back to her room after the big scene with Devante in the music room. At least that's what it felt like to her: a scene, a drama, a thing she needed to write about in her journal. But first, she needed a regular pencil or pen. Those, and the other things that had been declared off limits yesterday, had been returned to her after this morning's short session with Dr. Lutkin. She'd gotten everything back but her combat boots, which, she was told, she might get to wear again after she and Dr. Lutkin had their real session on Monday. She had to get everything out of the box and back where it belonged.

Just like every other Saturday, she was expected to clean her room so the counselors could come and inspect it. She wanted them to see that even though she had been on restriction last night, she was doing better now. And she definitely didn't want her parents to know. She didn't want to get caught off guard again in case they came in her room today. So she got to work. But she decided she wanted to listen to something while she cleaned.

She took her boombox out of the cardboard box and plugged it in. She put the tape her parents gave her in the tape deck so she could hear it.

"If I don't like it, I can always tape over it," she shrugged.

An off-key gospel choir started singing as soon as she pressed play. She never did trust her father's taste in music. She fast-forwarded past the music, getting to the part where the new youth pastor was preaching, and listened to him while she put the rest of her things away.

"Young ladies and young gentlemen, I'm sure from the time you were in Sunday School every adult you've come across has quoted a scripture to you, 'Children, obey your parents in the Lord for this is right.' Or maybe 'Honor thy father and thy mother and thy days will be long upon the Earth.' And those are important scriptures.

"But tonight I'm preaching to y'all from another text, from the New Testament. Tonight I'ma tell y'all about a young man about your age, only 12 years old. He obeyed his parents. He honored his parents. But then one day he had to stand up to his parents. And his name was Jesus."

Janina stopped unpacking and stared at the boombox, not believing what she was hearing. Somebody from her church was actually saying that? Then there was a knock on the door. It was Nurse Erica with a book in her hand.

"After I told Dr. Lutkin about what we discussed last night, he wanted me to loan you this," Nurse Erica said.

She handed Janina a book with a funny title, *Bringing up Parents: The Teenager's Handbook.* There was a Post-it note on the cover. Dr. Lutkin had written, "Time to stand up for yourself!" The Lord sure worked in mysterious ways.

~~~

Dr. Lutkin looked at his watch and told Gail it was time to wrap things up. They walked to the center of the circle of chairs, and Gail addressed the group.

"Everyone, we'd like to thank all of you for coming and sharing your stories. It takes courage, but we can all learn from one another. And remember that when we take good care of ourselves, we have the inner strength to take good care of our children."

As she helped Dr. Lutkin open the doors to the gym, Gail wondered if she'd said the right things. She hoped so. She felt like a fraud this morning, giving parenting advice when she had no kids of her own. But maybe that didn't matter. They seemed to like her. She hoped they did. She watched as they got up and helped themselves to refreshments. It seemed many had known each other for a while, and they broke up into smaller groups to talk. The Campbells shook hands with Mr. Monroe and Ms. Lewis.

"We haven't seen him since we brought him here on Monday." Mr. Monroe spoke forlornly of his son.

"It was the same way Janina's first week here. But now we get to see her all the time," Mrs. Campbell reassured him.

And just then, Mr. Monroe saw Devante at the doorway and waved to him. "Oh, there he is."

"And that's Janina right behind him," said Mr. Campbell.

"I see our kids have already met each other," Ms. Lewis smiled.

Janina wondered what conversation their parents were having about her and Devante behind those awkward smiles. And there was that new counselor, Gail, the one who had found her in the snow. What if she'd told her parents about it?

Devante wondered if his parents were still fighting about him. Walking from the doorway to where they stood, he felt his body clench with tension. But the tension vanished as soon as his mother wrapped her arms around him and gave him a big hug.

"It's so good to see you. How are you feeling?"

She searched his face for answers, just as she'd done that morning when she dropped him off at school.

"Better." He looked at the floor, feeling bad for what he'd put her through. Then he turned to Janina. "Oh, Janina, these are my parents."

She shook their hands, then turned to her own parents.

"Mama, Daddy, I really need to talk to you."

They said goodbye to Devante's parents and walked with her to a more secluded part of the gym where they could talk in private. And now she was alone with them. She was outnumbered. At times like this, she wished she wasn't an only child and that her parents hadn't come from such small and distant families, leaving their church members to become the surrogate relatives she wasn't sure she wanted. She thought of what the youth pastor said. Then she thought about what she'd just read in the book. She had to tell them how she felt, no matter how hard it was.

"I felt really hurt yesterday. And I felt humiliated when you yelled at me in front of everybody."

"Oh, Janina, honey, you know we really only want what's best for you," said her mother.

"And there was no need for you to get so emotional," said her father.

"But I can't help being emotional. What happened yesterday really hurt my feelings. And it's hard for me to tell you this, but it made me really angry, too. I felt like you were treating me like a little girl."

"But you'll always be our little girl, sweetie."

Her father just didn't get it. *I have to tell them how I feel,* she reminded herself.

"I feel like you're not really listening to me. What I'm trying to tell you is that I don't want you to treat me that way anymore. And also, I felt angry when you talked about Devante that way."

"Now that we've met his parents and heard their story, we see things differently," her father said.

"Our hearts go out to him and his family. I'm sorry we misjudged him." Her mother shook her head.

At least she was apologizing for what she said about him.

"I'm glad you see that now. But I feel like you've misjudged me, too."

"What do you mean?"

"Sometimes you treat me like I'm helpless and not capable of making my own decisions. Is it because I've been here so long?" Janina asked.

"We just don't want you to be overwhelmed," her mother said softly. "You take so many things so personally."

Janina's father reached down and stroked her hair in a gesture that seemed both tender and condescending at the same time to her.

"You're like a delicate little flower," he said in the kind of tone adults like to use when they talk to babies.

This was hopeless. Janina couldn't get through to them at all. Maybe they would never understand her. But maybe they could talk to someone who did.

"I think it's time we have another family session with Dr. Lutkin," Janina said in frustration.

Her mother was shocked.

"Janina! That's our decision, not yours."

In spite of this, Janina walked over to where Dr. Lutkin was talking with Gail. Janina's parents just stood and watched, too surprised to scold her.

"Excuse me, Dr. Lutkin, but I just had a quick question. Can you talk to my parents about having a family session? I tried standing up for myself, but they still don't seem to get it."

"Sure," he said. He told Gail he'd be right back, and walked with Janina over to her parents.

"It's been a while since I've seen you, other than in these meetings," he said after shaking their hands. "You know, Janina is really developing some great insight into her condition. And I think she's right. It's time we had another family session."

"Alright. How about next week?" said her father.

While her parents took out their day planners and checked their schedules, Dr. Lutkin looked at Janina and gave her a sly wink. They decided the session would be next Thursday, after her parents got off from work. It wasn't the triumphant victory Janina had hoped for, but it was better than being afraid of them. And besides, she hadn't had time to read more than a few pages of that book Dr. Lutkin had given her. She needed to finish it as soon as possible.

Wait a minute. Did he just get me to do homework, and make me want to hurry up and get it done?

Dr. Lutkin was already gone, talking to Devante's mom on the other side of the room.

"Here's the copy of the police report you asked me to bring. And I took pictures of Monica's house like you asked me to," Ms. Lewis said, handing Dr. Lutkin a large manila envelope.

"Thanks. These will be invaluable for the upcoming sessions. I'm going to have the photos of the house made into slides," Dr. Lutkin replied.

"Now that I've taken the pictures, I can't imagine how hard it'll be for him to look at them. Are you sure he's ready for this?" Ms. Lewis asked. She looked across the room at Devante, who was at the refreshments table with his father.

"We won't know until we try, but I'm feeling optimistic."

"Well, I trust your judgment. He's doing so much better since the last time I saw him. David and I are so grateful."

Across the gym, Devante spoke with his father and smiled. Ms. Lewis couldn't help but remember when she feared she'd never see her son again. She also remembered her fear that he would never smile again. This place was good for him.

CHAPTER 20
THE HUNGRY BRAIN

It was the first weekend she'd had in years. Medical school and her residency at Haven House had robbed Gail of her Saturdays and Sundays. But after the meeting with the parents was over, Dr. Lutkin had told her she wouldn't need to come back again until Monday. He'd even told her that he thought she'd established a good rapport with the group. Maybe her fears and doubts were unfounded.

She never would have guessed that this job, the hurdle Dr. Hoffman had placed before her, would turn out to be such a good experience. She had to let her know that it hadn't impeded her progress. She had to go and tell her face to face. So she went to the university hospital to see her.

"Things are going very well so far, and I wanted you to know. Thanks for giving me this chance. I'm learning so much from Dr. Lutkin."

The warmth of Gail's words seemed to thaw Dr.

Hoffman's cool reserve.

"I'm glad to hear that," she said with a smile, the first time Gail had ever seen that expression on Dr. Hoffman's face without a hint of sarcasm. "Listen, I know you and most of my other former students see me as a stern taskmaster who's never satisfied. But it's only because the quality of psychiatric care in this country is not as good as it should be, and your generation has the power to change that. I'm counting on you. Don't let me down!"

Then Dr. Hoffman's phone rang. It was an important call and couldn't wait. Gail understood.

"If Omar's out there, can you let him know I'll be a few minutes?"

Gail agreed to do it. She found Omar sitting in his usual spot when she left Dr. Hoffman's office.

"Omar, Dr. Hoffman wanted you to know she'll be a few minutes late. She had to take an important call. I see you here a lot. Are you working together?"

He looked up from the book he was reading, a medical text that Gail had read before with a great title: *The Man Who Mistook His Wife for a Hat.*

"Yes. Actually, we just got our research published."

"Congratulations! What's your paper about?"

"It's a topic of great personal interest to me, gifted children. Specifically, gifted children and how they can often be misdiagnosed with mental illnesses."

"Really?"

"Yeah, there could be thousands of gifted kids

out there right now who've been labeled with attention deficit disorder and even major depression, but the real problem is that their parents and teachers don't understand them. If you want to read our article, the library has a copy. It's in last month's *Journal of Child and Adolescent School Psychology*."

Gail took a little notepad out of her purse and jotted the name of the journal down in it.

"Sounds really interesting. I'll check it out."

Since psychology wasn't her major in college, she tried to read as many articles on the subject as she could. The more obscure, the better. She wanted to be prepared for anything. Her quest for knowledge about her field had made her an expert in her former university's library system. She went to one of the computer workstations and looked up Omar's article on a CD-ROM. It had a dramatic title: "Genius or Madness? The Misdiagnosis of Highly Gifted Youth." While she waited for the article to print, she did another search. Had Dr. Lutkin published anything? When his name came up as an author, she was surprised to see the category his writing was in. Not medicine, not psychology, but fiction. It was a story with a weird title in a magazine from Canada, "Angelhead" by Arthur Lutkin, Maple Leaf Literary Magazine, Windsor, Ontario, October 1978. She got the CD-ROM the story was on and printed out a copy of it.

~~~

"I really appreciate you coming on such short notice," Dr. Lutkin said to the young lawyer who had come to meet him in his office once the parent support group meeting ended.

"Anything for you, Dr. L. You saved my life."

Travis seemed an unlikely attorney, with his earring, ponytail, and tattoos. Oppositional, defiant, or in layman's terms, a troublemaker, as a boy he had gotten in trouble at home, at school, and everywhere else he went. In his time here, Dr. Lutkin, the teachers, and the other staff had helped Travis channel his rebellious ways into something more productive. His need to fight the system and his knack for finding loopholes served him well in his line of work.

After Dr. Lutkin's bold declaration in his meeting yesterday, Peter Roark whipped out his big black mobile phone, called up the Chief Financial Officer, and after a brief conversation, gave Dr. Lutkin an astronomical selling price. He did his best to appear unfazed as he did the calculations in his head. He had been frugal with the money Dr. Olmsted left for the school. But would it be enough? And could it even be used this way? Even his most desperately incorrigible patients had not prepared Dr. Lutkin for this encounter. But at least he had help. At least he knew a good lawyer he could rely on. He hadn't slept much last night. He kept crunching numbers and thinking of possible situations that could arise that could make the cost of operating the school go up. He'd have to find the money somehow, even if it meant paying everyone on staff their same salary while taking nothing for himself. He had some savings, and more importantly, prior experience in surviving on little or nothing. He'd do it again if he had to.

Rebecca had told him that The Harrison School would be nothing without PHEA.

"Look at all the referrals we've sent you. You need us."

But more often than not, the children PHEA had sent his way did not need to be at The Harrison School. The referrals made him think back to his late teens when he worked at a bookstore owned by a man who was sometimes called upon to do appraisals. Customers brought in old papers they claimed to have found in attics and basements, saying they were long-lost campaign speeches of obscure presidential candidates or early drafts of famous authors' Great American Novels. They brought them to the book dealer hoping to make a fortune on them. He would then invite Dr. Lutkin—who was still just Arthur back then—to look them over with him in the back of the store. And then the shrewd book dealer would show him all the evidence of forgery and fakery. It was very rare that anyone would come to the Greenwich Village bookstore with a genuine find.

He felt like his old friend the book dealer whenever PHEA sent him a potential patient. Janina was one of the rare genuine finds they had sent to him, perhaps the rarest of all. He was glad she her condition was improving since yesterday.

Looking up from the paperwork on Dr. Lutkin's desk, Travis explained, "The money Dr. Olmsted left in the trust can be used to buy this place back from those goons at PHEA. But it looks like you're about $150,000 short."

As he looked across his desk at Travis, Dr. Lutkin recalled a question that came up in a long-ago session.

"Do you live here, Dr. Lutkin?"

That wasn't the first time one of his patients asked him that question. Dr. Lutkin had smiled, remembering how ages ago as a little boy he too had thought that his teachers had a permanent residence in his elementary school. He had a theory that the blackboards folded out into Murphy beds at night. He didn't live here yet, but he would if he had to. This school had given him, much like its students, a special place to belong. He would do anything to save it.

"Know anyone who'd be interested in a condo in Lincoln Park? Because I know a very motivated seller," said Dr. Lutkin.

～～

Angelhead
by Dr. Arthur Lutkin

I saw the best minds of my generation destroyed by madness, starving hysterical naked,
dragging themselves through the Negro streets at dawn looking for an angry fix,

Angel-headed hipsters burning for the ancient heavenly connection
to the starry dynamo in the machinery of night...
—Alan Ginsberg, "Howl"

He *had* seen the best minds of his generation destroyed by madness. His own mind also was destroyed. All he had been told was that he had a nervous condition, with no specific definition of its cause or likely prognosis. That was all he knew when, as just a small boy—eleven, but small for his age—he was sent away to a foreboding ancient building that stood in somber isolation in the wilds of the Pacific Northwest. His parents had told him it was a boarding school. But it turned out to be a mental institution. He had come to this place for reasons unknown, his chief symptoms being daydreaming, stargazing, thousand-yard stares, distracting thoughts of the adventures of knights and castles, being picked last for every team, being too agreeable (though alternately too disagreeable), too sad, too happy, too angry, and too easy to overlook. All these traits made him a menace.

The alienation he felt from society was confirmed when his parents sent him away. He was not allowed to bring his toy knights or his books with him, though they were the only treasures of his lonely childhood. This was not a place to play games, and the orderlies made sure of it. Boyish outbursts were crimes to be punished with cold sheet packs and insulin coma therapy. His doctors were cruel men in horn-rimmed glasses dispensing medication with cool efficiency. The pills they gave him detached him from his own feelings and made him face each day with an unquestioning resignation. He was completely without initiative, and totally lethargic. He felt robotic. He felt empty. He felt drowsy and lousy. His doctors were pleased.

Then Paul buzzed in, high on uppers, a delinquent in a leather jacket. And he schooled Lance in the fine art of medication non-compliance. He banked their un-swallowed pills in a sock drawer.

"These are worth their weight in gold on the outside," Paul explained.

Lance's mind came back to life without the drugs to drag it down. Which meant drastic action from the doctors, who visited his temples with the sudden shock and awe of electricity. A morning without breakfast meant an afternoon of anesthesia and a night of headaches and burns from the paddles, and only remembering what had happened to him days later.

This went on until his parents made a fateful visit.

"Son, since nothing else is working, the doctors think what you need is a delicate brain operation. It's called a lobotomy."

When Lance told Paul the news, he said, "We need to split before they make a pod person out of you. Oh that's right, you haven't seen *Invasion of the Body Snatchers* yet. But you don't have to. Just look around."

Dead-eyed patients shambled around them, the lights in their eyes extinguished forever. Paul held up his bible—his paperback of *On The Road*—and told Lance, "This is what we gotta do. What this guy did."

They would get away like Jack Kerouac. They finagled a way to get day passes and never came back. Paul paid their way with pills that had been plucked from the mouth of madness. They had just enough bread for the bus to New York City. The boys thought they were hip to the scene, but Paul changed his tune. He felt like hitchhiking was a better way to get his kicks. After cooped-up years in and out of detention halls and mental hospitals, he wanted to see the country.

"I'm splittin' for Route 66," he told Lance.

But Lance stayed and became a student of Greenwich Village, triple-majoring in philosophy, poetry, and jazz. His classrooms, lecture halls, and laboratories were coffee shops, jazz clubs, bookstores, and poetry readings in crowded apartments. He found a job at a little place where the owner didn't ask too many questions and was willing to pay him in cash, a hole-in-the-wall bookstore and coffee shop called The Hungry Brain. It was there that Paul encountered the works of Sartre, Camus, and a far-out book called *The Mind That Found Itself.*

Seeing the cool cats wail on their saxophones and trombones every night made Paul yearn to express himself onstage. His time at the hospital had robbed him of the opportunity for musical instruction, so when he wailed with the band, his instrument was his mind. He hipped the crowds to his far-out angel-headed thoughts of kings and existentialism, knights and psychology, and mad minds finding themselves.

And one night after a rousing round of finger-snapped applause, a beatnik chick in the audience told him, "You're really tuned in, man! Where's your ivy tower?"

"I'm not in school," he shrugged. But he wished he were.

"A cat like you oughtta be a professor," said her goateed boyfriend.

And so he supplemented his Beatsville education with night school. He worried that his nervous condition might return. But his escape from Nutsville helped him shake it. And so ends the story of Lancelot, the angel-headed hipster kid with a hungry brain.

Gail pictured Dr. Lutkin dressed in a black turtleneck, beret, and sunglasses as he narrated the story. She'd grown fond of the Beat Poets when she first read their work as an English major. She was intrigued by the way that they had rebelled at a time in the 1950's when people were expected to conform. She liked the way they had drawn from Black culture, especially jazz, as a source of inspiration. In fact, from what she recalled, their attitude towards it was almost worshipful. When she finished reading the story, she wondered if Dr. Lutkin had been a beatnik.

It had been tricky for Janina to get away from her parents after the meeting this morning so she could have enough time to make Devante's present. Her mother really wanted to do her hair, but she didn't want her to see the damage the snow had done. She had styled it carefully to hide the frizziness that had resulted when her heat-straightened hair had met its enemy, water. She had no choice but to braid it again. But this time, she decided to have some fun with it, putting it in three braids that she twisted into knots that crowned her head, and letting two thin tendrils hang down from her forehead. She told Mama she could do it when she came back to visit next Friday. Making Devante's gift was more important, and she had to do it today so that the paint would be dry by tomorrow.

They had more free time on Saturday afternoons, and there usually weren't as many kids around. That was because many of them spent the afternoon off campus with their parents after the meeting was over, though of course Janina never did. After what happened yesterday, the counselors wouldn't have let her leave anyway. But it didn't matter. She was happy to spend her time in the art room instead.

Devante was still visiting with his parents. His mother had brought some things from home that she thought he might have wanted, like his CD player and some of his favorite tapes and CDs. She also brought some things he didn't want: a backpack full of school books and notebooks. His father had brought his teachers' lists of all the assignments he'd missed.

"Once you feel up to it," his mother said, noticing his immediate dismay.

"The most important thing is for you to get well," said his father.

It was nice to see his parents agree on something for once.

"Grandma is so sorry she couldn't come, but you know how hard it is for her to get around when the weather is like this. But she made sure I brought you a big piece of the sweet potato pie she made just for you."

Devante smiled, taking a foil-wrapped paper plate from his mother. Not even bothering to look for any utensils, he picked up the slice of pie like it was a slice of pizza and devoured it. It tasted like home. He hadn't realized he was hungry for it.

His parents left just before dinner. They had

kept the conversation positive and were careful not to mention anything that might upset him, though they did ask if he would mind if two of his friends came to visit. Chad and Jerome had been asking about him. He was surprised. He'd felt like they didn't want anything to do with him anymore. So he shrugged and said okay. They told him that his brother Derrick was planning to come, too.

Devante thought about what it would be like to see them again as he went into the cafeteria for dinner. He was sitting next to Janina. Now the other kids were looking at the two of them, dying to say something but forbidden because of the no teasing rule. Instead they talked about other things. There were rumors of a skating party.

"It probably won't happen, anyway," Ed grumbled. "Too many people are on restriction or just got off restriction."

The thing about being on restriction was that getting taken off was a gradual process. Just as Janina would have to wait to get her boots back, she would also have to wait before she could go on a field trip. Apparently Alejandra was on restriction right now. Janina wondered if she had tried to cut herself again.

"What a drag," Marcia sighed. "A skating party would've been groovy."

Maybe if Janina hadn't been on restriction last night, the counselors would have taken them on a trip to the skating rink. Now that Devante was there, she saw it as a chance to get to hold his hand again. It would have been so nice to have him beside her while a slow jam played, just as they had been yesterday before her parents interrupted. And she knew that Marcia would have loved skating to some old song from one of the records she picked up at the thrift store, with pictures of sideburned guys with long shaggy hair or big Afros and bell bottoms on the covers. Skating made Joey, who usually just sat in a corner and rocked back and forth, come alive. But her favorite person to watch at the rink was Ed. Once the counselors had helped him get over his fear of falling down, he was a natural. The way he moved made Janina wish there were an Olympic level competition for roller skating like there was for figure skating. It was one of the only things that seemed to make him happy, one of the only things that made Ed smile. Skating was one of the few field trips that everybody liked. And now they wouldn't get to do it. Something about knowing what could have been made it sadder, made her heart sink, made her eyes feel funny like she might start crying. But that was a dumb thing to cry about. Why was she so sensitive anyway?

Or maybe her sudden sadness wasn't caused by her craziness this time, but about having to say goodbye again as another kid left. Leon was going around to the tables where the other teenagers were sitting and letting all of them sign the goodbye book she saw him working on in the art room a few days ago. She hadn't known him really well. They weren't in the same groups, and he was in different classes since he was older, so the only times she saw him were at meals or else in art therapy. He had been   like Kathleen and Joey, out of touch with reality. But he had slowly gotten better. He would be going to college in the fall. Janina signed his book the way she usually did for the kids she didn't know well, wishing him a happy life in the outside world and dotting the "i" in her name with a little flower. But no one would ever remember her. Nobody would stay in touch. As soon as they left this place, as soon as they got back into their old routines or else started new ones, they left behind and forgot whoever remained at Harrison. She couldn't blame them. Why would you want anyone to be reminded of how crazy they once were when they weren't crazy anymore?

While he waited for Janina to sign his book, Leon introduced himself to Devante.

"Wassup. I'm Leon. Seen you around but never met you. I think you've got my old room."

"Nice to meet you," said Devante. "Good luck out there."

"Thanks. Take good care of my old room." Leon turned and looked at the rest of the group at the table. "So no skating tonight, huh? That's too bad."

Then Rod, one of the counselors at the table with them, perked up.

"Instead of skating, we're going to stay in and have a movie night in the lounge."

Everyone cheered up at the news, eagerly finishing their dinners and their nightly round of pills so that they could get back upstairs. Since it was Leon's last day, they let him choose the movie. He picked *E.T.*

Before starting the movie, Kirsten, one of the counselors told them, "Remember, guys, watching the movie isn't mandatory. If anyone thinks it's too scary or too much to deal with, you can go play Monopoly with Naomi downstairs in the playroom."

Devante thought she sounded like a misplaced kindergarten teacher. *E.T.* wasn't scary. It was just a movie for little kids. It was actually the first movie he ever remembered seeing in a theater, when he was only three. He was little enough to be scared of the alien the first time he saw him, until Derrick reminded him it wasn't real.

"We'll also have a discussion about it afterwards."

A discussion? But what was there to discuss? Devante kept his thoughts about how lame the whole thing sounded to himself. Maybe he was the only one who didn't see what the big deal was. Or maybe everyone else was too excited.

"I love this movie so much!" Janina whispered.

Rod turned off the lights.

"Are you okay with the lights being off?" Kirsten came over and asked Devante.

"It's cool." He shrugged, not wanting to admit that between the darkness around him and the darkness of the movie's opening scene, he felt tense.

He looked over at Ed, who sat beside him, wearing just one glove again. If Ed could brave the threat of germs, maybe Devante could defy the darkness. But when he saw the aliens for the first time, he jumped. He wasn't sure what embarrassed him more, that the counselors noticed, or that Janina, who was sitting on his other side, did.

She wondered what he was afraid of. He'd been acting nervous ever since the movie started. She wished she understood him better. She thought about their conversation this morning in the music room. She wondered who Monica was and how she had died. She was sitting closer to him than she ever had, but felt so distant from him. There was still so much she didn't know about him, but there were questions she promised she wouldn't ask.

It had been so long since Devante had watched a movie. In all the time he spent alone at home, he felt like he couldn't let his guard down, which was why he never even turned the TV on. But now he found himself really getting into this movie. He noticed that everyone else in the lounge seemed like they were really into the movie, too. By the light of the flickering television screen, Janina's dark eyes shone with tears when it looked like E.T. wasn't going to make it. And she wasn't the only one. Devante even felt tears coming on, though he did his best to will himself not to cry in front of everyone. It was hard not to. He knew exactly how Elliott felt when he told E.T. that he didn't feel anything anymore. There was so much more to this movie than he thought.

And then, out of nowhere, there were men

with big shotguns. He didn't remember there being any guns in this movie. He couldn't watch anymore. He turned away and covered his eyes. Maybe that counselor was right. Maybe he was just as helpless now as he was when he was three. He felt so small and so afraid that he was ashamed of himself.

"If you open your eyes now, you won't miss the best part," Janina nudged him.

The music soared as Elliott and the other boys took flight on their bicycles, evading the men with the guns. And for a moment, Devante felt like he was flying with them, too, carried away by the music as it rose higher and higher. For a moment, he was taken back to a simpler time in his life, when pedaling his bike as fast as he could with the wind in his face made him feel brave and unafraid of anything. His eyes watered as he wondered if he would ever feel like that again.

By the time the movie was over and the sad piano music was playing over the credits, he wasn't the only one who had shed some tears. While Rod turned the lights back on, the other kids were drying their eyes. Devante looked at their faces, surprised to see how openly they expressed their emotions, even the other boys. After all that group therapy, maybe they had gotten used to crying in front of each other. Besides a few subdued sniffles and the hum of the videotape rewinding in the VCR, the lounge had gone quiet.

"So, what did you guys think?" Kirsten broke

the silence.

Whenever Janina watched movies about aliens, she thought about how she used to daydream about being from another planet. It would explain so much, she thought. Of course, that was before she found out she was crazy.

Leon apologized for picking a movie that had made so many people cry. He said he'd chosen it because it was about going home and saying goodbye.

"I just wish E.T. was real," Marcia sighed.

A few of the others agreed with her.

"Who's to say he's not real?" asked Zack, his eyes full of suspicion. "What if there really are aliens and they're, like, watching us right now?"

With his questions, Zack had somehow managed to get everyone on the subject of the existence of intelligent alien life. Devante didn't want to talk about it. Instead, he wanted to talk to Janina about what she had done for him earlier.

"Thanks for not letting me miss my favorite part of the movie," he said to her quietly.

"You're welcome," she smiled.

The alien debate around them was getting heated, but neither of them wanted to get into it.

"So is this what you guys do here on Saturday nights, watch movies and talk about how it makes you feel?"

"Not all the time," she laughed. "But everything we do is therapy. I've been here long enough to figure it out. When we watched *The Wizard of Oz*, I told everybody how I never understood why Dorothy wanted to go back to Kansas because it looks so boring and it's not even in color. And then one of the counselors got all serious and was like, 'You know it was all a dream, right?' And I'm like, of course I know that! I'm not *that* crazy! I mean, at least I know the difference between reality and movies."

Catching herself, she covered her mouth.

"Oops. Glad nobody heard that."

She glanced guiltily at Marcia, who was caught up in the debate, then back at Devante.

"But you know the best thing about the movie, I think, is when E.T. came back to life. And I think I know why: The dry ice saved him. It was like being back on his home planet again."

"Oh, so you think he came from a planet made of dry ice? I never thought about that before, but it makes sense."

He would rather talk about what he thought about the movie than what it made him feel. His feelings were still far too exhausting to discuss, even with Janina. Besides, she probably had enough to deal with.

Despite what she had told him that morning about how much better she was now, he kept thinking of when he saw her yesterday, how small and helpless she had seemed. He wished he could forget the image of her dying in his dream last night. How much better was she, really? She wasn't wearing those knee high boots today. She had on shoes that buckled across the top, without laces. He watched as she opened her sketchbook and started drawing the very animated gestures Kyle made as he argued with Zack.

"So when do I get to see your graphic novel?"

"Oh, that's right! Sorry, I let Nurse Erica read it and she still has it."

"So you're done with it?"

"Not yet. This is how it works: I sketch everything out in this sketchbook, I write the story in another notebook, and then I put it all together in my good leather sketchbook."

He asked her what it was about, and she told him how she had gotten the idea for it, and how she thought it would be cool to create characters like her classmates, giving the fictional versions of them power to do things they couldn't do in real life.

"Imagine if a boy like Ed had telekinesis so he never had to touch anything," she whispered, "or if a girl like Kathleen could talk to people just by using her mind."

Rod and Kirsten had gotten the others to quiet down. Now everybody was watching Janina as she whispered into Devante's ear.

"What?" Janina asked, embarrassed.

It was impossible for all of them not to laugh. Even Devante was smiling. Janina smiled, too.

"All right, settle down," said Kirsten, who had somehow managed to keep a straight face. "It's time to get ready for bed."

Janina didn't want to go. She stood up slowly,

reluctantly, wanting to make the moment last. She looked at Devante and felt bad for him. She wished the present she had made him was ready now and not still drying in the art room.

"I hope you sleep okay tonight." She cringed at the emptiness of her words.

"Me too."

Then they headed in opposite directions, she to the girls' wing, he to the boys', where he took another sleeping pill and braced himself for the fearful dreams that were sure to come. Janina wanted Devante's face to be the last thing she saw before she closed her eyes. She opened her sketchbook to the page where she had drawn him and planted a soft kiss on his graphite cheek. It made her feel fluttery inside, like when she listened to Tevin Campbell. Finding the tape where she had recorded "Alone With You," she put it in her boombox. Then she took Snuggle out of the bottom drawer and reached inside the bear's stuffing for her headphones, but they were gone. Nurse Erica must have taken them. Why'd she have to be so thorough?

While Janina found it harder than usual to fall asleep without her favorite music playing, Devante was soon submerged in sleep and surrounded by all the frightful things that came with it. The next morning he woke up, startled, just as E.T. was trying to heal the gunshot wounds in Monica's liver and lungs with his eerie glowing finger.

He tried not to think about it while he ate breakfast. Janina was there with him, and so was

Alejandra, though she was too angry about her own problems to bother either of them. She had gotten off restriction just in time for their life skills activities.

"Life skills? More like life kills," Alejandra complained.

Devante had seen life skills on the schedule he'd been given, but didn't know what it meant. Janina told him that life skills was just a fancy name for cleaning up the bathrooms and the lounge and doing laundry. The boys and girls split up to do their chores, and Janina felt like she would never be finished. All she cared about was going to the art room and getting Devante's present. While she was scrubbing the colorful tiles around the shatterproof mirrors over the sinks, she heard Alejandra tell Heather and Raven why she had been on restriction last night, something about trying to run away so she could do ecstasy at a rave in a warehouse by the river.

"And Kirsten caught me and she was like, 'I'll run away with you.' Can you believe that? And then she took my glow sticks!" Alejandra went on when they were cleaning the lounge and Kirsten couldn't hear her over the sound of the vacuum cleaner.

Devante had come close to jeopardizing his new friendship with Ed when he almost used Ed's favorite washing machine. Fortunately Rod had intervened just in time. Now they were working together to arrange the lounge furniture exactly as it had been before it got rearranged for the movie last night. With all the real chores out of the way, Janina was finally able to go to the art room after lunch. She only planned to be there for a little while, but as usual, she lost herself in what she was working on.

When she got back to the lounge, Devante and Ed were playing Nintendo.

"Ed, I've never seen anybody play Dr. Mario like you. You've got mad skills. Think I'll take a break," Devante said, putting the controller down. Earlier that afternoon he'd figured out a way to trick Ed into using his uncovered hand when he challenged him to a free throw contest in the gym. It was hard to shoot one-handed, so Ed had no choice but to use both hands, especially since he wanted to do it perfectly. The contest had ended in a tie. Ed liked that because their scores were even. The only problem with Devante's plan was that Ed had felt the need to wash his hands for a long time afterwards. But at least he was using both of them.

Unlike the basketball, the controller didn't get bounced all over a gym floor, Devante had pointed out. Now Ed was playing with both hands on the controller, wearing just one glove. Without looking away from the screen, Ed said, "This is one of the only times when my OCD actually gives me an edge."

Devante stood up and saw Janina holding a shoe box in her hands. His name was written on the lid in a mixture of capital and lowercase letters in an assortment of hand drawn fonts.

"I made you a present." She smiled as she gave the box to him.

"What is it?" he asked as he opened it.

"They're stars you can put on your ceiling. They glow in the dark. I thought maybe if you were having a nightmare and woke up and saw them, you'd feel a little better."

Devante smiled. "That reminds me of that poem you were reading to me about the stars. Thanks."

She was so glad he liked them. She had seen some stars like that when she was on a field trip at the Planetarium. They sat down at a table together. He took a few of the stars out of the box and looked at them. They were a few different sizes and styles, covered in faint yellow paint, and flat on the back. Janina opened the book Dr. Lutkin gave her, *Bringing Up Parents*.

"What's that?"

"It's about how to stand up to your parents. Dr. Lutkin wants me to read it."

"He's got you doing homework, too? I thought you said the only homework here was getting better."

"It is, and I think this book could help me get better. What do you have to do?"

"Write a list of everything that gives me flashbacks. I still haven't done it yet."

"Why not?"

"First of all, why is he giving me homework in therapy? Isn't therapy supposed to make your life better? Homework only makes everything worse."

Janina laughed.

"Second, I'm scared to even write it. What if

just thinking about things that make me have flashbacks makes me have flashbacks?"

"That does sound scary. Why don't you ask him if he'll let you write it during your session?"

"Thanks. Good idea."

"There's a madness to my method, but there's always a rhyme to my reason."

"That almost made sense," he laughed.

She smiled.

"I think you hate homework even more than I did. I used to have a problem just turning it in. My teachers always made me feel like I couldn't do anything right," said Janina.

"I go to a magnet school, so I get tons of homework. It's still not good enough for my pops, though. He wanted me to go to private school."

"What's a magnet school?"

"It's a public school that's kinda like a private school because you have to take a test to get in. And the kids who go there come from all over, not just the neighborhood the school is in." Normally at this point, people would say things to him like, "You must be a genius or something," but Janina just smiled and nodded. He was glad she wasn't making a big deal of it.

"That's not too different from how things are here, when you think about it. I mean, some of the kids here came all the way from Wisconsin and Michigan. There was even a boy from Canada once."

Devante looked around at his new schoolmates, still feeling like a stranger.

"I never thought I'd say this, but I miss my school. I miss my friends. I don't know when I'll be ready to go back there, but Dr. Lutkin keeps telling me it won't be long."

"Really?"

"Yeah. He says maybe a month or so, depending on how things go."

"I'll miss you when you're gone. But I'm glad you're getting better."

"What about you? When do you think you'll be leaving? I mean, you've been here a long time."

"I don't know. Sometimes I feel like I'm gonna spend the rest of my life here."

They were so focused on their conversation that neither of them noticed the little boy who had escaped from the playroom. He ran through the lounge clutching a balloon, deftly evading the counselors and older kids trying to catch him and send him back where he belonged.

Devante was looking at Janina. He thought she looked like she was okay now and what she did on Friday never happened.

"What exactly is wrong with you, anyway?"

"Dr. Lutkin says it's a depressive disorder, 'not otherwise specified'. And that I have some features of schizotypal personality disorder and avoidant personality disorder. He's let me read some psychology books. It's like another language."

"You speak it well."

Suddenly, the little boy stomped on his balloon

and popped it. Devante was so startled by the sound that he screamed and ducked under the table. It sounded like a gunshot. He was so paralyzed by fear that he couldn't move.

"Are you okay?" Janina asked him.

But all he could do was sit there, frozen.

"Are you having a flashback? Can you hear me?"

He couldn't. In his mind he was on Monica's front steps, the gunshots echoing in his ears. It was all his fault. He could do nothing. He couldn't save her.

Janina tried what she'd seen Nurse Erica do. She crouched down on the floor beside him.

"You're safe now. It's okay," Janina told him again and again to reassure him. And finally he came out of it.

"What just happened? Are you okay?" Devante asked.

It seemed strange, and yet sort of thoughtful, that he was asking her if she was okay.

"Yeah, I'm okay. Are you?"

"I think so."

"It was just a little boy who popped a balloon. But he's gone now. They took him back to the playroom."

Now Devante could understand why Ed didn't like Fridays. Saturdays and Sundays were like that for him now. Too much wide open time on the calendar. Anything could happen. There were too many other people around, all those other kids, all those counselors. He needed to get away.

"I'm gonna go back to my room," he told Janina. "Want to come with me?"

They got permission from Tom, who stood outside the open door.

"Remember when you asked me what kind of music I liked the other day? I love good hip-hop. I like De La Soul, A Tribe Called Quest, Digable Planets, and KRS-One," he told Janina, showing her his tapes and CDs.

She had heard of most of them before, though the radio stations they usually listened to didn't play many of their songs that often. And then there were counselors who wouldn't allow the kids to listen to certain music (especially hip-hop) because they were afraid it would upset them. But sometimes the other kids in her mood disorders group would bring in songs they wanted to discuss: a guy singing about being a loser who deserved to be killed, a woman asking why people don't just crucify themselves, another guy rapping about his mind playing tricks on him. One time, Zack brought a music video about a boy named Jeremy who killed himself in front of all his classmates. It made Janina wonder about the mental health of the songwriters.

And then there was her church. They didn't want anyone to listen to any music that wasn't about God. She didn't know what the big deal was. What was so terrible about love songs? She liked listening to R&B groups like Boyz II Men, Jodeci, and En Vogue (and of course, Tevin Campbell), so she recorded their songs from the radio or made her own tapes from other kids' CDs and tapes. Having to sneak around so much to listen to music made her miss out on a lot of the songs other kids her age were listening to.

Devante put Digable Planets in his tape deck and began playing the group's most popular song, "The Rebirth of Slick." But as soon as he heard the first few notes, he could see Monica listening to it with him on his headphones. So he pressed the stop button.

"Sorry, I can't listen to it."

"Why not?"

"I almost had another flashback," he sighed. "But you can borrow the tape if you want."

"Thanks," Janina said. "Guess you should add music to your list."

"And balloons," he said with a smirk.

"Everybody's got something," she said to him softly. "We all have our reasons to be here."

"Yeah, I know." He shook his head. "I can't believe I was just talking about getting out of here when I can't even do something as simple as listening to music! I mean, music was my life. Now it makes me crazy. What should I do now, just sit and stare at the walls until Monday?"

"I think I know a place we can go that's quiet. You might like it."

She took him to the conservatory on the first floor. She was right. It was very quiet, like a library of plants, and flooded with golden, late-afternoon light. She showed him a green plastic flowerpot with her name on it. A little plant was sprouting in it.

"I'm not sure what kind of flower it's going to be. It's a surprise."

The occupational therapy teacher came over and introduced herself. "I'm Agnes. I see Janina's told you a little about the mystery seed project."

"Mystery seed?"

"Yes. You choose a seed at random from one of the packets I have, and plant it."

"I planted mine two weeks ago," Janina told him.

"It's ready for a new pot. It needs space for its roots to spread out," said Agnes.

She showed Janina how to re-pot the plant. Devante held the flowerpot as Janina carefully lifted it out. Wrapped solidly around a clump of dirt, its roots had taken on the awkward cube shape of the pot it had been in. Janina thought it would be funny if the leaves it grew were square shaped too. The fine white roots reminded Devante of angel hair pasta, and he suddenly felt his appetite returning.

The warm scent of the damp soil in the new, larger flowerpot made him think of his grandfather. Grandpa had hoped to share his knowledge of farming with all his grandchildren before he passed away, though his small city backyard was all he had. Devante remembered digging in the dirt with him, helping to plant vegetables and pulling up dandelions. He never learned all of what Grandpa had wanted to teach him about the life he'd given up so he could move up north to Chicago and work on the trains as a Pullman porter and fill in as a session musician on the side. But the scent of the earth was something that would always bring Devante back to those summers in the garden. And it was nice to remember something good for once and have a happy flashback so vivid he could hear Grandpa's hearty laugh.

Maybe he's keeping Monica company on the other side, Devante thought.

"Would you like to pick out a mystery seed?" Agnes asked him.

"Okay."

"Make sure it's something that grows fast. He's gonna be leaving soon," said Janina.

Dr. Lutkin could hardly believe his good fortune. Everything had happened so fast. After a few phone calls to friends of friends, Travis had found a buyer who was so eager to make the purchase that he came by to see the condo on Sunday and offered to pay in cash. Now Dr. Lutkin had until the end of the month to move out. The prospect of it didn't bother him, though. He had grown accustomed to it as a young man. As if he had anticipated a time when he would need to travel light, he had allowed himself to amass few possessions at home, so moving them would be easy. There was something romantic about the idea of taking what little furniture he had and putting it into storage, of existing primarily for his work and the here and now. He had traded his home for a cashier's check for enough money to make up the difference between the trust that had been left for the school, and what PHEA wanted him to pay for it.

Once the buyer left the conference room, Travis said, "I know that what you've shared with me about the school's financial situation is privileged, but there's a lot more I could do for you if you'd let me. There's a group of us still living here in Chicago and we get together sometimes. You've done so much for all of us. Let us return the favor."

"You really don't have to do that."

"I know. But I want to. You helped all of us so much. Let us help you now."

~~

Dear Shawn,

Today is my first full day working at The Harrison School, and I will probably spend all of it here in the break room, or, as my new colleague Carlos likes to call it, the break room that time forgot. They call it that because, unlike the rest of the school, this room was never modernized. It's a mixture of old furniture that doesn't quite go together, but it's all surprisingly comfortable, like the chair I'm sitting in now. Don't get me wrong, I'm not here because I'm not working. I'm in here because it is a good place to sit and read, and I will be doing a lot of that today.

When I got here this morning, Dr. Lutkin

called me into his office and told me something that I can't share with another living soul: all the patients here are part of an experiment. They don't know that the pills they're taking aren't real pills at all. They are placebos-pills that don't do anything. Sometimes we call them sugar pills, though they aren't always made of sugar. The ones at Harrison have vitamin C on the outside to make them taste bitter like real medicine. Carlos, who is also a pharmacist, makes them especially for the patients here. We use placebo pills in experiments. Sometimes this leads to what we call the placebo effect, which means that people taking the placebo pill start feeling better even though the pill doesn't do anything. It's a good way to test whether or not a new medication works. You have one group of patients taking the new medication and another group, the control group, taking the placebo.

Though the kids don't know about the experiment, their parents do. He said that many of them are actually grateful because their children already tried so many other drugs and had bad reactions to them, or have gotten no results at all. Then he said, how can we tell these kids to just say no to drugs, yet prescribe them addictive chemicals that alter their developing brains? How can we tell them they're too young to drink yet give them drug cocktails? How can we in good conscience give them medications that will stunt their growth, make it harder to learn, harder to remember, and harder to be creative?

The next thing he told me gave me chills. He said that these drugs are no different from a chemical lobotomy. A lobotomy is a really scary medical procedure that nobody really does anymore. It's a type of brain surgery, and when it goes wrong, it leaves people with irreversible brain damage.

"I took a Hippocratic oath not to harm my patients," said Dr. Lutkin. "And if I ever harmed a single one of them... God help me, I could never forgive myself."

I asked him why they would even bother with giving the patients the placebo drug, and then he explained that they were doing it for the money. Drug companies were paying them to participate in studies. They weren't getting enough money from the government to help keep their costs down, and he and Dr. Olmsted didn't want the school to become so expensive so that only kids from wealthy families could afford to be treated there. Dr. Olmsted sold the school to PHEA, that terrible company that also owns Haven House. I don't know how I could have missed that. Fortunately, the deals with PHEA and PharmaCo will all be over soon. So at least that's good news.

Dr. Lutkin's strong stance against giving his patients medications for their mental illnesses is going to make my job a whole lot harder. I don't know how to do what the other counselors here are doing. They're social workers or clinical psychologists who were trained totally differently from how I was trained in med school, but Dr. Lutkin is asking me to do what they do. From the state hospital to Haven House, all I have ever done is work with medicated patients. This is a new challenge for me and I don't know if I'm really right for this job. But Dr. Lutkin says he has faith in me, especially after what I did for Janina and the parents' group on Saturday.

He gave me the files of the patients he wants me to work with while I'm here. Janina is one of them. He said I should take some time to get used to the way things are done here and is allowing me to spend the day reading the files of my four patients and studying the books in the staff resource library, which is also here in the break room.

I wondered if his position on medication might have had anything to do with what happened to his brother, and so I asked him. He seemed startled at my question, and shocked that I had found the story he had written so long ago and published in such an obscure journal.

He went pale and just said, "Yes, what passed for treatment back then was horrific."

Then he complimented me on my observation and research skills and said he thinks I'll do an excellent job. I hope I can prove him right. I thinks that's why I'm writing to you now. All the years I studied psychiatry I thought that if I could have given you the right drugs, you would have calmed down and gotten better. I didn't think that just talking to you would have been enough. What could I have said? And what can I say to these new patients? I suppose reading their files is the best way to start. I better get to work.

Devante was nervous when he came to Dr. Lutkin's office for his first session of the week.

"I didn't do my homework for today," Devante said, looking down at the floor.

"Why not?"

"Okay, I know this might sound dumb, but it scares me. I still want to do it, though. But, but I thought it might be easier if I wrote the list in here," Devante explained.

"Sure. Take a seat."

Devante felt relieved. Maybe therapy homework wasn't so bad after all. Dr. Lutkin got up and took a blank notebook from his bookshelf and a pen from his desk, and gave them to Devante.

"You can use this."

Devante sat with the pen in his hand, too afraid to write.

"Try starting with the least threatening thing

first."

"Okay." He took a deep breath and began to write. "Red roses. White teddy bears. The dark."

Just saying the words and seeing them written on paper made him fearful, but he tried to add a few more things to his list.

"My grandma's house. Monica's house."

He stopped, too afraid to go on.

"Good work," said Dr. Lutkin. "Keep going."

He tried to compose himself.

"Blood. Guns. Cars slowing down in front of the house."

He put the pen and notebook down and started rocking back and forth and breathing hard.

"I know this is hard for you. Is there anything else? Is that everything?"

Devante wanted to stay calm. He didn't want to have a flashback. He didn't want to go crazy again, but he had to say it.

"Monica! Pictures of Monica! And the music we used to listen to." He started crying. "The music... Why is it always music?"

He used to hear music everywhere. He could find it in every sound, even ordinary things like dripping faucets, vacuum cleaners, dial tones and busy signals, windshield wipers, dishwashers, rumbling trains, car alarms, morning traffic, school bells, footsteps and sneaker squeaks, and people's voices. For him, everything used to have a tempo and a timbre and a tone. Then he heard the gunshots and the windows breaking and the sirens. After that, he couldn't hear the music anymore.

As his hands trembled, he said, "It makes me feel things. It makes me remember."

"What does it make you remember?" Dr. Lutkin asked.

"The way she used to sing. Her voice. She sang while I played the piano. It should've been me, not her. I was supposed to protect her. She took those bullets for me. Those guys were after someone else who was dressed like me. That's what the cops said later. I was in the wrong place at the wrong time. I should never have gone over to her house. It's all my fault."

He was breaking down now. He had lost it. He had never cried like this, not this much.

"What are you feeling now?"

"Like I'm about to go crazy. Like I'm gonna lose my mind!" Devante looked to the psychiatrist for reassurance.

"You're not going crazy. You're in a safe place." Dr. Lutkin pointed to the toy castle in the play area. "You see that little castle over there?"

"Yeah."

"Imagine that you're one of the knights in that castle. You wear a full suit of armor that protects you from your head to your feet. Imagine you live inside that castle, under the protection of your king. Imagine the other knights are your comrades in arms and you all look out for each other."

"Okay. I can imagine that."

"Good. How would that make you feel, to live that way, to be one of those knights?"

"Safe. Strong."

"You have that same strength inside yourself. You just told me a long list of your worst fears, and you didn't go crazy, as you put it. You're still talking to me, not hiding behind your silence. You still know who you are and what year it is, right?"

"Yeah."

"So could it be, then, that what felt like going crazy was really something else?"

Devante was starting to feel a little calmer now. "Sure. Carlos told me I might feel a lot of different things all at once."

"Yes. A powerful mixture of many conflicting emotions."

"You know, that's how I've been feeling since Monica died. Scared, angry, guilty, depressed, confused... It's just too many feelings to deal with all at the same time."

"Yes. And all those feelings are painful feelings. No matter where you turn, you're in pain."

Devante nodded.

"But remember your inner strength. Your work is to use that inner strength, to draw upon the healthy part of yourself as the part of you that was wounded by trauma begins to heal. It won't be easy, but all of us here in this castle are here for you, Devante. You've made a lot of progress so far. You came here of your own free will. You drew from your inner strength and chose to come here to get better.

"Keep that notebook. You don't have to read what you just wrote, that terrible list of fears. In fact, don't even look at that page. But use that notebook to write about your feelings so you can sort them out. And before you know it, you'll be ready to go home."

~~~

There really was no such thing as a "textbook case." For just as the Russian novelist Tolstoy had said that "every unhappy family is unhappy in its own way," Gail thought the same could be said of every unhappy teenager. She was sitting at a table in the break room, reading over the patient files Dr. Lutkin had given her. This was her somewhat belated orientation, getting to know more about Janina, Devante, Ed, and Marcia.

Marcia was not her real name, but that was what she wanted to be called. No, Gail realized as she read more, *needed* to be called so that she wouldn't be reminded about what had happened when she finally told someone at school what her stepfather had been doing to her. She had been the sole survivor. Her mother, sister, stepbrother, and stepfather had perished in the family station wagon as it idled in the garage. She was able to roll one of the windows down a little to get some air and honk the horn to alert the neighbors before succumbing to the carbon monoxide fumes. Her family tragedy had left her a ward of the state, and she was being treated for free. The school had set aside one bed per year for students who could not afford the cost of treatment.

Ed's obsessive compulsive disorder was so debilitating that he could not function at home or at school because of the many rituals he felt he had to perform. One of the counselors, a technology buff, was teaching Ed how to build his own computer, which was giving him a productive outlet for his perfectionism. But there was a debate amongst his treatment team over whether learning about germs in his science classes would make him more or less afraid of them.

Dr. Lutkin's notes on Devante's case were prefaced by a quote from a philosopher named Kierkegaard: "Anxiety can just as well express itself by muteness as by a scream." Devante had withdrawn from the world because he felt so overwhelmed by it, Dr. Lutkin had written. Devante feared being engulfed by his own emotions. But the progress he had made in his first week at the school was remarkable. And tomorrow he was to begin exposure therapy so that he could begin to cope with the trauma that had caused his acute stress disorder.

Dr. Lutkin had noted that Janina's depression was made worse by her focus on past disappointments and her emotional volatility. She had been withdrawn for a long time, hiding her true self for fear of ridicule and rejection, but the various therapies she participated in were giving her new ways to express herself and her feelings. He had poetically described the way he and the staff were slowly dismantling the walls she had built around herself brick by brick. He went on to say that she still showed highly unusual thought processes and extreme social anxiety, and they all agreed she should stay there until those issues were resolved. But she started showing improvement when she met Devante.

Gail thought about her brother again. The evidence of Shawn's illness had been there from the beginning, though no one had known it at the time. He was fearful and fretful and had a strange way of playing with his toys, preferring to sleep with a hard metal roller skate Gail had outgrown rather than a soft stuffed animal. His teachers had said he was "slow." Gail felt she'd failed him as an older sister when she tried to teach him new things and he would respond by whimpering, "I can't. It's too hard!" So many things seemed to confuse him. A puzzled frown was the signature expression on his face, and she often worried about him. But her parents were always hopeful that he'd outgrow it. They all learned too late that their hopefulness had been a form of denial, and that Shawn's condition had been gradually worsening. If only she had known then what she knew now about child development and the early signs of schizophrenia. Because of what happened to Shawn, she would take no sign or symptom for granted now.

At another table, Erica was trying to read something, but Carlos kept reading over her shoulder.

"I'd tell you to get your own copy, but this is the only one," Erica said to him.

"Will you let me read it when you're done?" asked Carlos.

"You've already read most of it over my shoulder so far," she laughed, "but I'll ask Janina if she doesn't mind letting you see it."

"It's just so good. So interesting! The evil psychiatrist who's experimenting on the kids in the basement looks kinda like Dr. Scratchansniff from *Animaniacs*," said Carlos, a little embarrassed that he'd just admitted to watching kids' cartoons in his free time. "And I want to find out what happens to that poor little lab mouse, Sparky."

"I don't know what doctor you're talking about, but I think the girl who can start fires with her mind looks like Alejandra."

"Yeah, you're right." Carlos chuckled. "It's a good thing Alejandra can't start fires with her mind. This place would be burned to a crisp."

Erica laughed. Gail looked up from the files she was reading. "What are you guys talking about?" she asked.

"This comic Janina's been working on. It's awesome. You know, she's our resident artist," said Carlos, who had become familiar with Janina's work after finding her sketchbooks in the lounge a few times.

Erica let Gail take a look at the graphic novel. The drawings were very well done.

"Incredible. She did this all by herself?" Gail asked.

"Yes, she's been working on it for about a year now. Her teachers even let her work on it in class as a creative writing project," Erica explained.

"She should get it published. She's such a great storyteller," said Carlos. "And you can tell she's done some research. She knows what neurotransmitters are."

"If her depression and shyness weren't holding her back so much, she'd be unstoppable," Erica sighed.

"Carlos, when you're done, I'd like to read it," said Gail.

She pulled out Janina's file again. It was such an unusual case, but Gail thought that maybe reading her graphic novel might help her understand Janina better.

꙲

"For the first time, I realized what everybody's been telling me about anger and depression. It really is turning my anger inward and back at myself."

Janina was having her first session of the week. Dr. Lutkin was smiling as he took notes. Maybe she'd get her boots back after all.

"Good. And did you realize what you were angry about?"

"Yeah. My parents, of course. They treat me like a baby. You know what my dad did when I saw him Saturday? He patted me on the head and told me I was a delicate little flower. I hate it when he talks to me like that! I'm fourteen, not four. But even when I was four, I hated being treated like I was four. I don't know why."

"Perhaps because you wanted to be taken seriously."

"Yeah, maybe that's it. I hate being bossed around and having people talk to me like I'm stupid just because they're older than me."

"Is that what you feel like your parents are doing?"

"Yes. And I am so glad that you and that new counselor didn't say anything to my parents about... you know, what I did on Friday." Janina felt too ashamed to look Dr. Lutkin in the eyes when she brought it up. "I'm feeling a lot better now than I did then. Do you think I'm getting better?"

"Yes, definitely. Other than your setback on Friday."

"I just wonder if I'll ever be normal. I wonder if I will ever fit in out there. I wonder if there's any place where I belong. Everybody thinks I'm weird."

"Everybody?"

"Everybody out there, at least." She pointed at one of the windows. "You know what happened the last time I spent a week at home. I had a new friend for three days, but only because she just moved in and hadn't met the other kids yet. As soon as they got out for summer vacation, they told her all about me going to the loony bin. They called me names and threw things at me."

Just thinking about it again brought tears to Janina's eyes. Dr. Lutkin gave her a box of tissues and didn't say anything else until she dried her eyes.

"But that was only one girl, Janina. There are plenty of other kids out there. Making new friends isn't always easy, but it's not impossible. After all, you just made a new friend last week."

She smiled. "I really like Devante. But when he gets better and leaves, he'll probably forget about me. I wish I could leave when he leaves and then we could see each other all the time."

"Well I'm not sure exactly when he'll be ready to leave, but you still have a ways to go before you're ready."

He was telling her exactly what she didn't want to hear. Ever since Devante had let her borrow his Digable Planets tape the other day, she'd been listening to it. The way they rapped about New York City made her wish she could go and see it. They said it was like a museum with its posters and graffiti. But now, who knew how long she'd have to stay here? And she had brought it all on herself.

"I know. What I did last Friday was so stupid," Janina said.

"You're beating up on yourself again," he interrupted her. "You know what that means."

"Homework?"

"Yes. You've got to write down those negative thoughts as soon as you think them."

"And then write down whether or not they're

true?"

"Exactly. I'm glad you remember this exercise. But you need for it to become more than just an exercise you do because I tell you to do it. It needs to become a part of your own thought process.

"What happened on Friday really concerns me. What if Gail and I hadn't been passing by? What if no one had come? We all care so much about you, Janina. You also must learn to care about yourself. You need to learn to forgive yourself when you make mistakes. That's what you've really been struggling with all these years.

"But you've also made a great deal of progress. What you did on Saturday was proof of how far you've come."

"You mean standing up to my parents?"

"Yes, that's exactly what I mean."

"But they didn't understand what I was trying to tell them."

"That's okay. You just keep trying. And we'll help you."

Janina was glad they would help her, though she wished she didn't need any help. Them helping her meant that Meredith and Kirsten would no longer let her go down to the first floor without dressing appropriately for the weather, even though she wasn't planning on going outside. She had to wear her sleeveless and short-sleeved dresses with a long-sleeved shirt underneath or a jacket or sweater on top, and leggings, too. It meant not being allowed to use the sharp scissors to cut fabric in occupational therapy without Libby watching her like a hawk.

Why couldn't she be normal? If she could be normal, she could have a normal life. Maybe she could even be with Devante. But then again, would her parents even let her have a boyfriend once she went back home?

"What's wrong?" Dr. Lutkin could read the sadness on her face.

"It's just..." She started crying again. "Devante. I'm gonna miss him so much. I think I'm falling in love with him."

After giving her a moment to dry her tears, Dr. Lutkin told her, "Before you can love anyone else, you have to learn to love yourself."

~~

After spending most of the day cooped up in the break room, Gail felt like she needed a change of scenery. So she paid a visit to Janina's second-floor classroom once classes were over for the day.

"I'm trying to get the full picture of who my new patients are. Can you tell me how Janina is doing academically?"

"She's doing exceptionally well," Matthew, Janina's teacher, said. "I'm not sure if you're aware of this, but she can read at a college level. She's really benefiting from the individualized instruction she gets here. Every day when Janina comes to class, we let her draw and write a story, and once she's gotten that out of the way, she studies other subjects."

Matthew took a book report from his desk and showed it to Gail.

"Here's a report she just turned in. Look at how she designed the cover."

The elaborately illustrated cover depicted a man and a dog in a barren, snowy landscape. In fancy hand-drawn lettering, Janina had written the words "To Build a Fire".

"I think I remember that story. Isn't it about a prospector who froze to death?" asked Gail.

"Yes, it's a classic by Jack London."

Gail thought of the day she had found Janina shivering in the snow, and wondered if she'd been inspired by this story. It gave her chills. Sure, academically Janina could handle this material, but was it too much for her emotionally? Was her psyche too fragile? Would she have been better off reading Dr. Seuss or *Where's Waldo* like the kids at Haven House?

Still, she thought as she went back downstairs to the break room, the fact that the girl was so intelligent seemed to complicate matters. She thought about Omar's article, which she had read yesterday. She had brought it to work with her today, hoping to re-read it at some point. She skimmed through it until she found the part she was looking for.

"Children and adolescents who are creatively gifted are especially at risk for misdiagnosis because of their highly unusual thought processes."

Wasn't there something similar in Janina's file? Gail looked back through the pages and pages of detailed notes taken from four years of sessions. There was something at the beginning, from when Janina was ten years old: "Patient exhibits unusual thought processes and excessive social anxiety." And then Gail noticed something else. There was an intake form that showed that Janina had been referred to Harrison by her former school, Precious Angels Christian Academy. Did Omar's theories apply to Janina's case? Gail decided she'd go and talk to Janina's old teachers. The phone number and address of the school were listed, so she copied them down.

∿

After everyone else in his firm had gone home, Travis met with a small group of his fellow former patients in the conference room. All of them were now in their twenties and thirties and believed they'd only made it to adulthood because of what Dr. Lutkin and his school had done for them.

"We all need to call at least five other people from Harrison we're still in touch with," the lawyer said. "Simone, when the letters start coming in, hold on to them so he can get all of them at once."

Simone said she couldn't wait.

BRIGHT STARS, DARK FLOWERS

I hope nobody else will read this. Dr. Lutkin, my shrink, says I don't have to show this notebook to anybody, not even him, unless I want to. Writing is supposed to help me figure out how I feel.

How I'm feeling. . . That's complicated.

This might sound kinda wack, but sometimes I think the real reason I wanted to live in my grandma's neighborhood is that I thought it would be like a rap video. I thought there would be rap battles and DJ contests and barbecues every day. There was so much I didn't know. Everything was so different from where I grew up, in Beverly in a house on a hill on Longwood Drive. When I was little I used to visit Grandma's house all the time, but the neighborhood has changed a lot. My mother blames it on crack dealers and crackheads. She grew up there, and she's been trying to do what she can to save it from becoming a ghetto. That's why she moved back after the divorce. And I moved there because I couldn't stand being around my dad. We have nothing in common. It's hard to believe I'm his son sometimes. Then again, it's hard to believe my parents were even married once. They _really_ don't have anything in common! One time after they had a huge argument, I asked my brother Derrick if he could tell me the reason they got married in the first place. And he said, "You're looking at him."

But since I've come here, things are getting a little better with my moms and my pops. When they first got divorced, I didn't know whose side I was on half the time. It seems like when your parents split, you're split, too. But now there's a lot less fighting about me, and a lot more communication. Even my pops is making an effort. We had a family session today and it went pretty well. There's a lot to talk about because there's so much stuff I never told anyone about. It was too overwhelming. Dr. Lutkin said that I was isolating myself from people.

I guess I didn't know what else to do. There was too much happening and too much to deal with, and I felt like I was going crazy but I was scared to tell anyone. And I thought my pops would be like,

"See, I told you so" because he wanted me to go live with him in his new condo downtown and go to some private school where I'd have to dress preppy and cut my hair and quit listening to hip-hop since he thinks it's not respectable. In other words, he wants me to be just like Derrick. And my moms already has enough to deal with since Grandma had a stroke and can't get around like she used to, plus she's busy with all her meetings and helping people who can't afford a lawyer but really need one. And Derrick is away at college now, and Chad and Jerome don't really understand what happened because they weren't there. So maybe I already felt isolated.

Really, to be honest, I didn't feel much of anything at all. I was so numb most of the time. Nothing seemed real anymore. Every day was just like another nightmare. Then I tried to go back to school, and all I could think about was wanting to die, just let death suck the life from me like CPR in reverse. Two times this year, I've stared death in the face. Both times death has taken me to the window, but not to the door.

When I listen to music, I don't feel numb. And when I play music, I don't feel empty anymore. And when I listen to the music that Monica and I used to listen to, I feel like she can hear it too. When I talked about it in group today, Scott said that was no reason to stop listening to it. He said not to avoid the memories. He even had Tom go to my room and get some of my CDs. I had to pick a song to play for the group. And when it started playing, I cried in front of everybody. I could picture Monica listening to it with me.

She loved music just as much as I do. And she had such a good voice. You know how most of the time you hate it when people sing along with the radio because they ruin the song? Well, when Monica sang along, she made everything sound better. She had so much going for her and so many plans and it pisses me off that she'll never get to do any of the things she was dreaming of. Mostly I'm mad at myself because those guys were shooting at me. I had the same Jordans and Starter jacket and Bulls hat as the dude they were looking for. If it hadn't been for me, she'd still be alive. I shouldn't have gone over there that night. How could I have been so stupid? Had my back turned to the street and everything. Every time I think about it, it makes me furious.

I'm finding ways to get my anger out. My girl Janina told me that keeping your anger inside can make you depressed. In fact, I just got back from beating up a punching bag in the gym. It felt so good to just pummel it over and over and over again.

Yesterday my brother came by for a visit and brought Chad and Jerome with him. It felt kinda weird letting them see me like this, but it was good to know they hadn't forgotten about me while I've been here. Derrick came back in town just to see me. He told me Dad's been telling people that I'm on a study abroad trip in Europe, which made Chad and Jerome laugh since they heard rumors that I'm down south visiting my relatives on my mom's side. I guess nobody wants people to know where I really am. After all, we're the kind of family where everything is such a big secret. No one is supposed to know the truth, not if it makes you look bad. And what could make you look worse than having a crazy son or brother or friend? They all said my secret is safe with them. Then we talked about other stuff, like the Bulls. It was kinda awkward.

And Derrick said he was impressed by the size of my room. He says it's bigger than his dorm room, which he has to share with 2 other guys. I think they all were surprised that there were no bars on the windows and I wasn't tied up in a straightjacket or wearing a face mask like dude from "Silence of the Lambs" or something. Oh, snap! Wasn't that guy a shrink? I don't think I could watch a movie like that again for a long time. We watched

E.T. over the weekend and I couldn't handle it. Can't watch movies, can't listen to music, but Dr. Lutkin keeps talking about me going back home. How can I even do that when I'm always buggin' out about something?

I wish I could stop having nightmares. I wish I could stop being so scared. Could I wish on a star for that? If only it was that simple. But Janina made me some stars that glow in the dark, and I put them on the ceiling over my bed. My boy Ed helped me. He wanted them to be perfect. He was trying to line them up like the stars on the flag. I tried to tell him that they wouldn't look realistic that way. I mean, if the real stars were all perfectly aligned, we wouldn't have constellations. Then Ed offered to go get a book about constellations so we can make it accurate and I was like, let's just make up some of our own. Eventually I convinced him and now my ceiling full of stars looks tight. When I wake up and look at them, it makes it easier for me to go back to sleep, no matter how bad the nightmare might be. And it beats having a nightlight like I'm a little kid.

It helps knowing that I'm not the only one who feels this way. I can share things in group and the other kids really get it. When I'm there, I feel accepted and understood.

But when I'm with Janina, my feelings aren't complicated at all. I just feel happy. I think she has pretty eyes. But lately, every time I see those pretty eyes, they're red with tears. One time I asked her if something was wrong, but she said she was fine. I get it. Sometimes you just don't want to talk about stuff.

~~~

I don't know what to paint anymore. Philip, my art teacher, says it's not about just making a pretty picture, but painting what I feel. All I know is I don't feel like finishing the painting I started the day I met Devante because everything was different then. Now all those bright colors are meaningless to me.

In the back part of the studio, where they keep the clay, Devante was trying out the potter's wheel for the first time. He was making a mess, but having a lot of fun doing it, like a little boy making mud pies. In fact, he was covered in mud from the wet clay. He even managed to get a little in his hair somehow. He looked so cute. Then he started laughing. I had never heard him laugh so much before, and when I looked over at him, I couldn't help but laugh, too. I was glad to see him smile. But soon he'll be gone.

Devante is getting better. But getting better means saying goodbye. Soon I will be helping him make his goodbye book and signing it before he walks out of the door and out of my life, possibly forever. But of course I want him to get well again and stop having nightmares and feeling guilty for what happened to Monica. I remember what he was like when I met him last week. That's no way to live. But to stay here without him? That's no way for me to live. And I don't know how much longer it's gonna take for me to get well. I wish I could be normal, but I don't belong anywhere but here. Dr. Lutkin said I'm so busy anticipating how I will feel when he's gone that I'm not enjoying the time we still have together.

I can feel my heart quietly breaking. But I have to bear this tragedy alone. I can't shed any more tears about it where people can see me, not in group, not with Dr. Lutkin. I have to show all of them that I'm stronger than that. I am not my father's delicate little flower. I am not the same girl I was last Friday in the snow. And besides, I made a promise to Devante. I also made a new deal with Dr. Lutkin. I don't want him calling my parents.

Lately I've started to feel like there are too

many colors--in my clothes, in my room, in this school. I had to get rid of them. So I made some black and gray flowers, and then I managed to sneak a bottle of black paint and a little paintbrush out of the art room so I could paint all the butterflies and flowers on my wall black and gray.

All my life I've told myself that I'm okay with being alone. But now that I've finally made a real friend, I dread being lonely again.

CHAPTER 25
SUFFER THE LITTLE CHILDREN

Gail hoped that the drive out to the south suburbs would be worth it. She was on her way to her appointment with Reverend Weaver, the principal of Precious Angels Christian Academy, Janina's former school. She wondered if she was asking the wrong questions and seeing something that wasn't there because she hoped there'd be a mystery to solve. She hoped not. At the same time, part of her hoped that she was wrong.

The school was on the same block as the church affiliated with it. The building was quiet when Gail got there, except for an off-key gospel choir rehearsing somewhere. School was out for the day. Through the transom window above the principal's office door, she could see the words "Suffer the Little Children" in bold letters. She went in and introduced herself to Reverend Weaver. Interesting. The psychiatrist in Janina's graphic novel had the same last name.

"Thanks for taking the time to meet with me today," Gail said as she shook his hand.

"No trouble at all, my sister. Now which former student did you have questions about?"

Gail noticed another quote on the wall, a plaque that said "Spare the rod, spoil the child." Hanging on a hook below it was a wooden paddle, the kind that was used for corporal punishment. Gail looked back at the Reverend.

"Janina Campbell. She left four years ago."

Reverend Weaver shook his head.

"Oh, yes, Janina. She's Deacon and Missionary Campbell's daughter. We are still praying that God will heal her mind. Most of her teachers are still teaching here. I'll take you around and introduce you."

"I really appreciate this. I'd like to speak with them one on one, if that's alright."

"Sure. Anything I can do to help."

Reverend Weaver explained that they taught students from preschool all the way through the twelfth grade as he led Gail down the hall to the first grade classroom. Peeking into the trophy cases in the hallway, she saw photos of the students. All the girls were dressed in the dowdiest, most drably colored uniforms she had ever seen. And it seemed the highest prize was the Most Obedient Student award, a tall gold trophy that bore the inscription "Obedience is better than sacrifice."

"She was always in her own little world," said Janina's first grade teacher. "I couldn't get her to stop staring out the window. After a while I would tell her since she liked looking out of the window so much, she should go stand next to it. She spent a lot of time standing by that window when I had her that year."

"Janina? I don't remember her. Janina, Katrina, Sabrina, Christina... All those little girls' names sound the same to me," said Janina's second grade teacher.

"Oh, Janina! Yes, I do remember her. That was the girl they called the space cadet, unfortunately." Said Janina's third grade teacher. "She was always daydreaming, so we'd say, 'Earth to Janina' to get her attention. We watched the launch of the *Challenger* in science class, and when it exploded, she cried about it for weeks! I told her crying wouldn't change anything, but she was inconsolable. The kids all started calling her a crybaby."

"She wasn't very coordinated," said the gym teacher gruffly. "I had a hard time getting the other students to let her play on their teams. When they played softball she'd sit out in left field and play with the dandelions in the grass. Just daydreaming. Almost got hit by a pitch one time."

"When I asked her why she was drawing in my class, that girl had the nerve to tell me she was bored." Janina's fourth grade teacher was still bitter about that, apparently. "It's not my job to keep her from getting bored. I'm an educator, not an entertainer!" Though with her face heavily coated in quantities of makeup that rivaled what televangelist Tammy Faye

Baker wore, Gail thought the teacher looked like she was made up for a camera crew.

"Janina was one of the most talented students I ever had," said the art teacher. He took an old handmade card out of his desk and showed it to Gail. "I still have this card she gave me before she went away. It's hard for me to look at it. I feel so bad that we didn't do more for her."

"They let her skip preschool and kindergarten, but if I had my way she would have repeated the fifth grade," Janina's fifth grade teacher said, her arms folded across her chest. "If she's so smart, why couldn't she follow directions? She always had to find another way to do things. And she was always drawing pictures instead of doing her work! I tried to teach her some discipline by having her write 'I will follow directions' one hundred times and hand it in. And you know what she did? She wrote 'I am stupid and I hate myself' one hundred times and handed that in. Just hard-headed!"

The school librarian was an older woman with a kind face. "Well, I know I wasn't supposed to," she said softly, "but I let her come in here and read during recess sometimes. Janina loved books. She used to sit right over there by the aquarium and read. She'd get so absorbed in reading that I had to remind her when it was time to go back to her classes. I didn't want her to get in any more trouble, poor thing. She didn't seem to have any friends. Once, she told me that the books and the fish were her friends."

"I have zero tolerance for students who don't

pay attention," Janina's sixth grade teacher said sternly, punctuating his words with the tap of his wooden pointer in his open palm. "I caught her drawing pictures in my class time and time again. I tried everything, confiscating her drawings, taking away her art supplies, talking to her parents, rewarding the other students who told on her, but nothing would stop her. Near the end of the school year, I called her up to my desk and I told her I was going to send her to the principal's office to get paddled. And I will never forget what Janina did after that. She just stood there right in front of me and started slapping herself in the face and calling herself stupid. So I sent her to the counselor's office instead."

The school counselor's desk was covered with promotional items from PHEA. The coffee mug, pencil cup, and the pencils in it all had the PHEA logo on them. Gail could see a resemblance between the guidance counselor and the brainwashed nurse Janina had drawn in *Psindrome*.

"The girl was at risk. She isolated herself from her peers, she lived in a fantasy world, she wasn't focused on her schoolwork, she didn't turn in assignments even though she had completed them, she kept having emotional outbursts, she started acting out in self-destructive ways... I knew she needed help. So I referred the Campbells to PHEA."

"I noticed that a lot of the things on your desk have their logo on them." Gail tried to keep the accusation out of her voice. And then she saw a tacky picture frame that said "Bahamas" on it, with a vacation photo of the counselor inside. For a moment Gail wondered why tourists always brought back the ugliest souvenirs from the beautiful West Indian islands that her family had come from.

"Oh yes, PHEA was mighty good to me in those days. You know, they even had a raffle for staff who gave them good referrals. That's how I won my trip to the Bahamas, all expenses paid! What a blessing!"

A blessing? It sounded more like bribery to Gail. And she was glad that PHEA didn't have such "special relationships" with school counselors anymore. As she walked back to the principal's office, she thought of the paddle that hung on his wall, and of the teachers who were willing to use it. It was one thing to discipline a child in a way that would teach her to have self-discipline, and another to systematically break her will. One thing to foster her self-discovery and another to break her down in order to build her up in someone else's image. And Janina clearly didn't fit the image that most of her teachers expected her to have. It explained a lot.

"This has been very useful. Thanks again," Gail told Reverend Weaver.

"You're welcome, sister," he said.

She didn't want to say the wrong thing, but she couldn't leave without telling him what she thought.

"I know I'm not an educator myself," Gail told him as she put on her coat, "but if I can be candid for a moment, I wanted to tell you that I'm very disappointed that so many of your teachers seem to have let their personal feelings about Janina get in the way of their responsibilities to her. But since it's too late for Janina, I hope you'll talk to them about being more professional with the students they have now."

The look that Reverend Weaver gave her after she told him this was heavy with remorse.

On her way back into the city, Gail thought over what she had just seen. She let it all sink in and tried to make sense of it. She had gotten everyone else's opinions of her new patient, but what she needed most of all was to hear from Janina herself.

Janina's turtleneck was black. Her jeans were black. Her shoes and socks were black. And she had even painted her fingernails black with some nail polish she'd borrowed from Raven. Janina's hair was parted in the middle and pulled back into a tight bun. She sat at the table with Devante, about to have breakfast, not sure how many more times she'd get to do this. But before she ate her cereal, she folded her hands and bowed her head in a silent prayer. No one had ever seemed to notice her doing this countless times before, but Devante did.

"While you're at it, pray for me," he said. "The session I'm having with Lutkin today has got me buggin' out."

And so she asked the Lord to be with Devante in his session today, keeping her eyes closed longer than she needed to because it kept her tears from spilling.

Devante felt like he needed all the prayers he could get. His stomach was in a knot of anxiety. He wouldn't be able to finish his breakfast. All through his classes he dreaded the session, his mind too consumed with his fears to concentrate on making up the assignments he'd missed from school. He couldn't conjugate any of the new Latin verbs he was supposed to be learning, and he caught himself re-reading the same paragraph from *The Great Gatsby*. He looked at his math homework. $Y = mx + b$. There was something vaguely reassuring about equations. They were predictable. Maybe his life had too many variables and not enough constants.

By lunch the stress and dread had made Devante too queasy to eat, so instead he got a glass of ginger ale from the nice cafeteria lady Ed had introduced him to. And though Janina was sitting across from him, she seemed to be a million miles away. The way she was dressed today and the way she wore her hair made her look older now, and so did the serious expression on her face. She was so busy working on her graphic novel that she hardly seemed to notice him or anyone. She'd been like this since their classes this morning. She had a lot on her mind. Her story was almost over.

Steffanie and Tevin turned and looked at each other. What could they say now that their prayers had been answered? The people around them gathered in front of the news cameras, eager to comment on what had happened though they scarcely knew the story. In the meeting room, the press conference had broken up, and the future of the night was uncertain.

"Talk about putting a damper on things." Tevin laughed to himself. "Guess we got all dressed up for nothing."

"But we won, Tevin! And that's all that matters!" Steffanie reached down for Sparky's cage. "You hear that, Sparky? We won!"

But he wasn't moving. Tevin opened the cage and took Sparky out. The mouse's body was rigid and cold.

"I don't think he's breathing, Steffanie."

How could this be happening? Everything else had worked out.

"He probably got hurt while we were running with the cage." Tevin put his other hand on Steffanie's shoulder.

"Sparky, wake up! Wake up. You're so cold."

"Let's put him back in the cage." Tevin wrapped the cloth around Sparky's whole body, head to tail, and gently placed the mouse on the wood shavings of the cage floor.

"What happens to me now?" Steffanie asked Tevin.

"I have no idea," whispered Janina to her characters, putting down her pen with an ink-stained hand.

Devante looked up from his math homework, wondering who Janina was talking to. A glance at the clock told him it was almost time for his session. His teacher let him leave class early so he could go. He felt like he might throw up on the way there, but luckily, he didn't. When he got to Dr. Lutkin's office, a new counselor was with him.

"I'm Gail," she said. "I'll be helping out with your session today."

"Now what you must understand, Devante," said Dr. Lutkin, who seemed to have sensed his anxiety, "is that both of us are here for you, no matter how difficult things get."

Gail fixed her gaze on the nervous young man. She felt a little nervous, too. There was considerable risk with this sort of intervention. She and Dr. Lutkin had already discussed how careful they would both have to be. Seeing the pictures they were going to show Devante today was certain to induce flashbacks. Dr. Lutkin had warned her that this would not be like the movies, when a single therapy session spent reliving some terrible trauma was so cathartic that the patient was spontaneously healed. Working with Devante would be a process, like a slow surgery on a patient who was fully awake the whole time. And no matter how much it tested her own endurance, Gail needed Devante to know from the very beginning that she, too, was his ally.

She had him sit in a chair facing a blank

expanse of wall. Dr. Lutkin had taken down the medieval tapestry that had been hanging on it. He closed his shades to darken the room, then turned the lights off.

"I'll be right here beside you the whole time," Gail promised Devante as Dr. Lutkin turned on the slide projector.

Much to Devante's relief, nothing appeared on the wall in front of him but a bright square of light.

"I'm going to show you some pictures," said Dr. Lutkin. "When you look at them, I want you to tell us what memories they bring up for you, okay?"

"Okay," said Devante nervously. His heart was pumping so hard that his entire field of vision seemed to throb.

Devante looked so shaky and unsteady that Gail wondered if they should be doing this at all. Still, they had to try. If things went well, this session would help him make sense of what he had experienced. What if he couldn't handle it and ended up hyperventilating, fainting, or—nauseated as he looked—vomiting? If only she could give him some anti-anxiety medication, just enough to take the edge off. But of course, that wasn't an option. Dr. Lutkin's words from yesterday came back to her: "*You* must be his anti-anxiety medication." It certainly was a lot to ask of her. But she had to try.

"You feeling alright?" she asked Devante.

"I feel kinda sick, actually."

Gail had prepared for this session by learning

everything she could about breathing techniques for relaxation, even asking Anjali what helped her patients when they were in labor.

"I want you to try something. Sit all the way back in your chair and take a deep breath, and don't breathe out until I tell you to."

He did as he was instructed.

"Good. One more time," said Gail.

Doing it a second time quieted the storm in his stomach.

"Very good. Now do it again."

When he did it a third time, Gail saw his neck and shoulders relax.

"You ready now?" She didn't want them to start a moment too soon.

"I think so. At least, I don't feel sick anymore."

"Good," said Dr. Lutkin. "Here's the first picture."

With a click, the projector advanced, and the front of Monica's house appeared on the wall before him. Too scared to cry, too terrified to scream, Devante stared at the scene of the crime. Sure, it looked like a traditional brown brick Chicago style bungalow to anyone else, but he could still see it cordoned off with yellow crime scene tape. And then he saw what it looked like when the tape came down and the blood was scrubbed from the steps and neighbors had left flowers, stuffed animals, and candles.

"What's coming up for you?" asked Dr. Lutkin.

In that moment Devante was flooded with

memories, and then he was back there on the porch, time traveling back to that dreadful night. Everything was coming up for him, maybe even what little breakfast he'd eaten, since stress always went straight to his stomach. The picture on the wall was churning up sickening memories. Bitter words rose in his throat like bile and he heaved them out into the silence of the room as his heart pounded and his fingers trembled. He spewed out a steady stream of visceral descriptions of the horrors that poisoned his mind until there was nothing left for him to do but gasp for air.

"Deep breaths now," said Gail, one hand on his back. "That's it, just breathe. Good."

Once his breathing started getting back to normal, he realized he didn't feel like throwing up anymore. Gradually he realized where he was. The ordeal was over, and he was safe—for now.

"Okay. That's enough for today. Good work," said Dr. Lutkin.

Gail turned the lights back on as Dr. Lutkin shut the slide projector off.

"You made it!" Gail congratulated him. "How are you feeling?"

"Just glad to get it over with," Devante said hoarsely.

"I think you've made enough progress now for short visits off campus. So the next time your family or friends stop by, you can take a little field trip if you like. Just let one of the counselors know first."

After what he just went through, spending

time with his family and friends outside of the school for a few hours sounded great.

"Cool."

"Since today's session was so intense, let's end a little early."

Devante looked relieved. Gail was glad to see the expression on his face. It was definitely not like a scene from a movie, but progress nonetheless. She realized it would be a slow unburdening that took place over the course of a series of sessions.

When Devante got up from the chair, he seemed to stand a little taller, and move with a greater sense of purpose. He thought about going back to the room that had all the plants in it. He needed to be someplace quiet. On his way there, he saw Janina in the hall.

"How'd it go?" she asked him.

"It was crazy intense! I'm so glad I made it through. I'm gonna have to do it a few more times before I'm ready to go back out there and see the house again. Depending on how it goes, they might let me start going back to my classes. I'd still spend the night here until I'm ready to go back home again."

Janina felt tears welling up in her eyes. She tried to rub them away before he noticed.

"Are you crying? What's wrong?"

"I'm... just... happy for you." She felt bad for the half-truth she told. "Sometimes I cry when I'm happy."

But from the look on her face, Devante wasn't convinced those were tears of joy. Before he could say anything else, Janina said, "I have to go see Dr. Lutkin real quick. I'll talk to you later."

After all, they had a deal.

∿

Gail hoped that between the two of them, she and Dr. Lutkin had written down everything Devante had told them. The words had come pouring out of him so rapidly, and they needed to use his account of the events, as well as what they gleaned from the police report, to help him process his memories in a more constructive way. She and Dr. Lutkin would have to compare notes.

"Good work today," Dr. Lutkin said to her. "I have a meeting soon, so you can come back when I have my next session in an hour."

"Okay," said Gail as she picked up the files she wanted to study during her break. She wanted to make sure she hadn't missed anything in Janina's file.

Dr. Lutkin opened the door to let Gail out and Travis in. As soon as Dr. Lutkin closed the door, Gail saw Janina heading in her direction with a mournful expression on her face.

"I just missed him, didn't I?" She asked Gail. "I really need to talk right now."

"You can talk to me," Gail told her.

"Okay," said Janina, disappointed.

Maybe she could give Gail a chance. After all, she had kept her promise not to tell her parents about last Friday. She had even asked Janina if she could read *Psindrome* when Nurse Erica was finished with it.

"Where would you like to go?"

"We can talk in my room," Janina replied.

When Janina opened the door to her room, Gail thought it looked different somehow. Yes, it was darker. Before there had been a riot of colors, some so bright they might have glowed in the dark. Janina looked somber in black, the curator of her gallery of gloom. She sat down on her bed and Gail pulled up a chair beside it.

"Nice flowers. Did you make them?"

"Yes, with tissue paper."

Intrigued, Gail gently took one of the paper flower petals between her thumb and index finger.

"Feels thicker than tissue paper."

"That's because I painted them, and the paint stiffened them. They're not as delicate anymore."

"It looks like you've had a lot of time to make flowers in art therapy. You've been here quite a while, haven't you? Four years. What's that been like for you?"

"I like it here. Everyone's really nice. People don't laugh at me like they did at my old school. Nobody makes fun of my crazy ideas since everyone here is crazy, too." Janina didn't want to talk to Gail about Devante. Maybe she shouldn't have gone to see Dr. Lutkin. Maybe she should have just waited until tomorrow. And maybe she shouldn't have painted her nails black, she thought as she stared at them. Nail polish remover was hard to come by at this place.

"I had a chance to talk to some of your old teachers," Gail told her. Janina looked up at Gail, stunned. Nobody had ever gone to talk to her old teachers before. "Why do you think you had such a hard time at your old school?"

The school counselor had said Janina couldn't come back to Precious Angels until she'd gotten better. There was a part of her, she realized just now, that didn't want to get better if it meant having to go back there.

"I was drawing and daydreaming in my classes. But it was hard not to because they were all so boring. I was finished with my work before the other kids, but I got in trouble if I decided to read the next chapters in my books on my own. They always told me I was being disobedient. And if you're disobedient at that school, they can punish you with the paddle. Eventually I realized that they won't punish you if you punish yourself first."

"How did you punish yourself?"

"If I did something stupid and they made me write lines, you know, like repeating 'I will pay attention in class' a hundred times, I'd write 'I am stupid' a hundred times. I thought that would show them how bad I felt for what I did. Or if they were getting ready to use the paddle, I'd hit myself before they could hit me."

"Sounds like going to that school was very painful for you, both emotionally and physically."

"It was. But maybe I'm just too sensitive."

"What makes you say that?"

"Because I cried too much. It just gave the kids another reason to make fun of me and the teachers another reason to yell at me. Everyone here says that there's nothing wrong with crying, but out there, I don't think people see it that way."

"Did you ever talk to your parents about going to another school?"

"Sometimes. But they didn't want me to. They liked Precious Angels because a lot of people from our church go there."

"Oh, so you saw the same kids on Sundays that you did all week long?"

"Yes. Saturdays too, if they were coming to Mama's salon to get their hair done."

"Is that what a typical weekend was like for you, then? Saturdays at the salon and Sundays at the church?"

Janina thought about Sundays when she still went home, her parents making her get up in front of the entire congregation so the pastor could lay hands on her and pray for her healing. She could still feel the flare of hot shame beneath her skin as she felt herself being watched by all those pitying eyes. She remembered feeling embarrassed to see her name on the prayer list for "sick and shut-in" members in the church bulletin. Something was wrong with her and all of them knew. Now she wished she had asked her parents to let the pastor pray for her in the church office instead of in front of everyone.

"Yes, that was my weekend until I stopped going and just stayed here all the time instead."

"So you wouldn't have to deal with all those kids making fun of you."

"Yes."

"Thanks for helping me to get to know you better. We met so abruptly last week. Would it be okay if I asked you what happened out there in the snow?"

"Sure. I was feeling depressed, although later I realized it was caused by internalized anger at my parents. But at the time I didn't know that. I just felt ashamed of myself. Whenever my dad says he's disappointed in me, it breaks my heart."

"Did you feel like you should be punished?"

"Yes. I felt like I deserved to suffer."

"You just read a story about a man who froze to death, didn't you? So you knew how dangerous it could be."

"Yeah, it sounded terrifying. Jack London tried to make it sound like it wasn't a bad way to go, but it scared me."

"So then why did you go out there if it scared you? Did you want to freeze to death?"

"I wanted to punish myself. I wanted to see how long I could take it. But I didn't want to stay out there too long because the snow would mess up my hair once it melted."

"So then it wasn't a suicide attempt?"

"I thought it was basically the same thing as suicide." Janina shrugged. "Not that it really matters.

It's a symptom of my depression. It was a crazy thing to do, but I do crazy things because I'm crazy."

As Gail looked at Janina, she thought about some teens she'd seen on their way to the mall the other day, bareheaded and glove-less despite the chilly weather. A glance at their designer footwear told her they weren't dressed like this because they couldn't afford winter clothes. They were just more concerned with the cool factor than the wind chill factor. If they were at Harrison instead of Water Tower, would she see them differently?

"What about the reason your parents brought you here?"

"You mean when I was ten? With the compass?"

Janina remembered the scent of her suburban bedroom in the summertime. It was almost the end of the school year, her last year at Precious Angels. She remembered kneeling on the floor beside the foot of the pink canopy bed, the point of the compass stabbing through her drawing right down to the plush mauve carpet. So many feelings. Fear, anger, maybe something else.

"It was a really morbid thing to do."

"Were you thinking of stabbing yourself?"

"I was thinking about something that happened at school."

"Were they going to punish you again?" Gail asked.

All the tears that Janina had been trying to hold back came pouring out of her. "They were gonna make me repeat the sixth grade."

Suddenly she was reliving it all, the pain, the humiliation, the anger at herself but not her teachers. Her sixth grade teacher was the worst. He patrolled the aisles of his classroom with a wooden pointer in his hand, demanding that all the students address him as "sir." She couldn't say she hated him. That would be a sin. Instead, as soon as she got home she had drawn a picture of him holding his stupid wooden pointer with a stupid look on his stupid face and tore it up into tiny little pieces.

She sputtered out sob-choked words. "And... the... counselor... said... I had to come here. And I... hated... myself... and all my... stupid drawings!"

She remembered placing the self portrait she had done in art class on the floor on top of the shreds of the picture of the teacher she despised. What good was drawing? All it did was get her in trouble. She remembered her colored pencil eyes staring up at her blankly from the paper as she plunged the needle-sharp compass point between them.

"My... mother... walked... in..."

Janina drew her knees up to her chest and buried her face in them. Gail stood up and put her arm around Janina's shoulders.

"I... just... want... to be normal," Janina wept.

She had been praying to become normal for so long. It was the only prayer that never seemed to get answered.

CHAPTER 27
MEDICAL DETECTIVE

Gail hoped she hadn't been too forceful in her questioning. She felt like she had pulled a string and kept unraveling Janina's defenses until they had all come undone. But she needed to pull that thread, that continuous line of questioning, to get to the truth. Janina's words were haunting. So all along, she had been trying to punish herself. And all along she had been misunderstood by all the adults and all the professionals around her. Misunderstood by her parents and teachers, turned over to a school counselor who would be rewarded with a free vacation for sending PHEA another child who didn't need their services, but had excellent insurance coverage. But how could this be? How could this have happened to Janina? And what was Dr. Lutkin's role in it?

Both Dr. Hoffman and Omar were eager to talk to Gail about Janina's case. Gail used the time that Dr. Lutkin had given her for patient research to go and meet with them at Dr. Hoffman's office.

"I've been reading your article, and I think one of my patients has been misdiagnosed. I just spoke with her teachers and it's clear that none of them understood her. Her school thrives on discipline and obedience, and she is a bright girl with the soul of an artist who needs to be free to express herself."

"That kind of environment could destroy a child like her."

"Tell me about it! This school is so strict, they even punish the children physically. From what I understand, her parents sent her there because it's affiliated with the church they attend. But now that she's at Harrison, she's doing very well academically because her teachers work with her one on one. She's fourteen years old and reads at a college level. Dr. Lutkin's official diagnosis for her is depression, but I think her old school caused it."

"Sounds like the school I went to before my parents realized I was gifted," said Omar.

"What's worse, she was referred to Harrison by a counselor at her school who got kickbacks from PHEA, which owns Harrison now. And I already know from working at Haven House that many of the kids they admit don't even need to be there," Gail continued.

"Have you shared your concerns with Dr. Lutkin?" Dr. Hoffman asked.

"No, not yet." Gail cringed at the thought of making a mistake. "I wanted to be absolutely certain and eliminate all doubt before I go to him with this."

"There will always be something to doubt. One of your greatest strengths is your willingness to ask questions, dig deeper, and search for answers. But once the detective work is over, you need to trust yourself with the answers you've found."

"It's gotta be hard to know when to stop looking for evidence," said Omar. "In many ways, your field is still rather primitive when you compare it to other areas of medicine. You don't get to confirm a diagnosis with an x-ray or biopsy. You could even say psychiatry is more of an art than a science, really."

"That's why getting a second opinion is so important. And Arthur's a reasonable man. He'll listen to what you have to say," Dr. Hoffman said.

"I hope you're right."

Gail still felt uneasy about confronting him, though she didn't know why. Maybe it was because of what he had told her about his brother.

"Did he ever tell you about his brother?" she asked Dr. Hoffman.

"I never knew he had a brother," she said, sounding surprised. "We dated in med school, but there was so much he never shared with me. I never even got to meet his family. Why? Was there something—"

"Never mind," Gail said, feeling a little embarrassed that she had put Dr. Hoffman on the spot like that. She never knew there was a history between the two of them. "It's probably not relevant anyway, and I feel like it isn't my place to share what he told me."

Dr. Hoffman looked wistful for a moment, then said, "Now Dr. Thomas, one thing to keep in mind in cases like this: you need to approach this with an open mind. If this girl truly has been misdiagnosed, then that means that for the past four years, everything she has said or done has been seen by the people around her in the context of the labels she's been given. She may have even come to see herself in the same way. The good thing is you haven't interacted with her long enough for those labels to truly stick."

Then Omar said, "The thing we seem to forget about labels is that they can come off."

CHAPTER 28

TALKING TO MYSELF ON PAPER

I felt sick all day because I was so scared that I'd go crazy in my session. They showed me a picture of Monica's house, and it was like the whole thing was happening all over again. I felt like I was there and I could see everything just like the night it happened. Experiencing it again like that was just as bad as the first time, but talking about it helped me to get it out of my system. When they turned the lights back on, things seemed different somehow. Not like I'm 100% back to normal, but like I'm a lot closer than I was last week. Still, I was glad they let me leave early. I needed some time alone to think and not have to talk to anybody, so I went back to the greenhouse to check on my plant. The seed already sprouted, even though I just got it on Sunday. That was fast. Then I had a group meeting, and after that it was time for dinner.

When I saw Janina in the cafeteria, her eyes were so red and puffy. I asked her what was wrong, and she told me how scared she is that she will never fit in once she gets out of here. She told me that she hasn't gone home with her parents in two years because the kids in her neighborhood always made fun of her. So I told her about the kids in the neighborhood where I grew up. We were the second Black family on our block. I'm glad we weren't the first. My mom always talks about how hard things were for her and my grandparents since they were the first ones to integrate her block in the 60s. Our neighbors never threw bricks or burned crosses, but they had other ways of showing us that they didn't want us there. I told Janina about the kids whose parents would let me play in their yards but not inside their houses, the times Derrick got pulled over by cops in the neighborhood for driving Dad's BMW, and the nosy lady on the corner who asked Grandma if she was a maid because good domestic help is so hard to find. In spite of it all, I met Chad and his family. They've always been cool with us. Then when I moved in with Grandma, a lot of the kids in the neighborhood made fun of me because I'm from Beverly. They said I wasn't really from the South Side (even though Beverly is just as far south as Grandma's neighborhood), and that I thought I was better than them. But then I met Jerome.

And I told her she's gonna meet somebody like that one day. I mean, she's such a great person, and I can't see why anyone wouldn't want to be friends with her. I've never met anyone like her before, but that's what I like about her.

~~~

I could avoid him. I could abandon him before he abandons me. But I don't want to. Maybe I'm not good at endings. Or maybe it's because for the first time I feel like someone my age actually understands me, and I don't know if it will ever happen again. He said it could. And when he said it, he reached across the table and put his hand on mine, and it was like that day when we were dancing. Only more bittersweet than that. It was a reminder of how little time we have left together here. But at the same time, my heart was racing, and I felt like my entire nervous system had been replaced with a string of multicolored blinking Christmas lights. He is the only boy who has ever made me feel that way.

And when we talked, I realized something I didn't before: He is a normal guy who was traumatized.

But me? Well, I think my brain is wired wrong. I've read a few psychology books now, and they say it could be the chemicals in the brain that make people crazy. Maybe there are two kinds of kids at this school: the ones who are wired wrong and the ones who were wronged. Or maybe four kinds of kids: the sojourners, who only stay for a little while, and the ones like me who stay for years & years. And I happen to have fallen in love with a sojourner. What I need to do is to try my hardest to get better so I can get out of here & live a normal life. I told the new counselor about it, and she says she's gonna help me.

~~~

Dear Shawn,

Nagging thoughts are making it impossible for me to sleep tonight. I could be wrong. I could be applying what I learned in the most recent article I read to a case that has nothing to do with it. What if Janina was lying about wanting to punish herself? What if Dr. Lutkin is right and Janina really is depressed? After all, she changed the decorations in her room. She took all the colorful flowers and butterflies on her wall and painted them black and gray.

Even with Dr. Lutkin, I'm starting to get the feeling that things aren't what they seem and he's hiding something from me. It seems pretty strange that he never told Dr. Hoffman about his brother, even though they dated for a while in medical school. Why would he keep that from her? Was he ashamed? Why would he be, when they were both studying to become psychiatrists? I don't think it's anything to be ashamed of. I'm definitely not ashamed of you. The only reason I was so hesitant to talk about you during my interviews was that I didn't want to become overly emotional. It's kind of ironic when you think about it, but even though my job is to help other people express their emotions, I am supposed to stay in control of my own at all times while I'm working.

After a restless night and anxious morning, Gail finally had a chance to talk to Dr. Lutkin in the afternoon. She caught him right after Rebecca, Peter, and Travis were leaving his office.

"Dr. Thomas! You're just the person I wanted to see. I'd like you to be the first to know that The Harrison School is officially free of PHEA!" Dr. Lutkin said triumphantly.

"I'm glad to hear it," said Gail, wishing she could be more enthusiastic. But this was not the time for that. "I need to speak with you right away. It's urgent. It's about Janina. About her diagnosis."

He let her into his office and nodded to his assistant before closing the door.

"What is it?" He looked very concerned.

"First, I think you should take a look at this journal article Dr. Hoffman just published." Gail had made another copy of it yesterday, just for Dr. Lutkin.

"'Genius or Madness'? What's this all about?"

There was no way to break the news gently, so Gail got right to the point. "I think you may have misdiagnosed Janina. I don't think she needs to be here."

"I don't understand. You've read her file. You've had a session with her. The first time you met her she was trying to kill herself."

"Actually, she wasn't. When we talked yesterday, she explained that she was trying to *punish* herself. She thought freezing to death would be frightening. What we saw wasn't what it looked like."

"But what about her other symptoms? Her depression, her unusual thought processes, her social avoidance?"

"What if her unhappiness was a normal reaction to an unhappy situation? I think that what we saw as depression was really a reaction to her environment. I went to her old school and talked to her teachers. They didn't understand her and the way they treated her led her to be ostracized by her peers. And she spent a lot of time with those kids, not just in school, but weekends, too. So of course she doesn't want to leave this school. Janina thinks that all she has to look forward to is teasing and humiliation. And it's all because her teachers didn't know how to work with a student as gifted as she is."

"It doesn't explain why she continued to experience symptoms of depression after coming here."

"Every day she's been a witness to one person's suicide attempt, another one's self-harm, another one's psychotic break. She probably couldn't help but wonder, 'what if I'm next?' But should she? What if her extreme emotional states are completely normal for her? All this time they've been treated as a symptom of an illness when they might just be a feature of her giftedness.

When I looked through the counselors' notes in her file, I noticed a pattern with her moods. They always dropped after her group therapy sessions. She seems sensitive to the feelings of those around her. I think she picks up on their pain very easily."

Raising his index finger as if to count another symptom, Dr. Lutkin said, "I also had to consider her odd behavior."

"Is it odd that she acts that way, or just a part of her creative process? Is she talking to herself when she's alone in her room, or just thinking out loud?"

"Even if that were so, she still has other issues."

"Her entire identity has been defined by her diagnosis. She takes the stigma of having been labeled wherever she goes. Even now the big issue seems to be going home. And why? Because of how everyone there has treated her. It's like she has been growing up in a fishbowl, always being observed, always encountering the same people again and again. Sadly, few of them seem to understand her. Wouldn't you agree that her anxiety about her environment is completely reasonable?"

"Yes, but the archetype of the tortured genius exists for a reason. It's completely within the realm of possibility for her to be both intelligent and depressed. The two are not mutually exclusive."

Gail was frustrated that she wasn't getting anywhere.

"There's no denying her intelligence. She's put things about neurotransmitters in her graphic novel. How many psychiatry books has she read?"

"I've loaned my books to her on occasion. They help her understand herself better, as well as her classmates."

Hearing him say this made Gail think about how she became a hypochondriac her first year of med school.

"But you know what can happen when you read about different symptoms. It's so easy to diagnose yourself with something you don't have, perhaps even think you're dying. Reading about anxiety can make you feel nervous. Reading about depression can make you sad."

"True, but there are still other features, including her uneven development."

"That's common in gifted children. They may be highly intelligent, but they still only have the emotional maturity of children."

Dr. Lutkin picked up the brass plaque with the Kerouac quote and traced its edges with his fingers.

"Since I began my practice I've encountered patients on occasion who were brilliant but lacked awareness of other people's emotions. They also lacked vital social and communication skills. We didn't have a name for their disorder, but now we do: Asperger's Syndrome. Actually there had been a name for it all along, but Dr. Asperger's findings hadn't been translated from the original German for decades—until now. So you see, it's quite possible Janina has a disorder that has yet to be named."

"If it's a disorder at all."

"I'll take a look at the article. It's a lot to consider. But you have to understand, hers is a very unusual case and I've only seen one other case like it before."

Gail felt disappointed, and it must have shown on her face because then Dr. Lutkin said, "You've obviously given this a great deal of consideration before coming to me with your findings. All I ask is that you allow me some time to read this article thoroughly."

There was a soft knock on the door. Dr. Lutkin went to see who it was, and found Simone there, her arms full of envelopes.

"Excuse me Dr. Lutkin, but I've been sitting on this and I couldn't hold on to it any longer. I've got something I think you should see."

The interruption was doubly disappointing for Gail. Would he even have time to read the article now? Simone had given him a big pile of letters to open.

"I'll leave you to your mail," she said as she left his office.

As Gail closed the door behind her, Dr. Lutkin took the letters and sat back down at his desk to open them. All of them were from his former patients.

Dear Dr. Lutkin, all the letters began...

When I heard about the school's financial situation, I knew I wanted to help. After all, my college is always asking me for donations. That's right, I said college. Can you believe I went to college? Remember how depressed I was when I was 17 and tried to kill myself because I was afraid I wouldn't get accepted?

I am now studying forensic psychology so that I can help other kids who were victims—I mean survivors—of kidnappings.

When I was 16 I came to your school because of my eating disorder. You helped me learn to love my body just the way it is. And now I am about to go on my first photo shoot as a plus-sized model!

My first tattoo was a picture of the Harrison front gate so I can always remember how safe I felt there.

Remember how I used to be afraid the

government was spying on me? Now I'm working for them! I'm a consultant for President Clinton on mental health issues.

If it wasn't for you, I don't know where I'd be today after the repeated abuse I suffered in foster care. Now I'm much better at protecting myself. In fact, I'm a third degree black belt in karate and I just opened my own dojo.

Every letter Dr. Lutkin opened had a check enclosed. Many also had pictures of his former patients as adults, posing with their spouses and children.

You taught me things I'm teaching my own kids.
Your school took me in when my parents didn't know what to do with me.
You accepted me as I am. No judgment. No shame.

There was a final letter to be delivered, and Simone needed only to read it aloud.

"I was so angry and tired of living, but you and Dr. Olmsted never gave up on me. You came to check on me every time I was on restriction. When my illness was tearing my family apart and my grandfather said that what was happening to me was proof my parents should never have left Korea, you were there for me.

When you visited me in the hospital after I graduated from here, you gave me hope to keep going. When you came to the halfway house and offered me this job, you gave me a place to belong."

Simone left Dr. Lutkin's office smiling. He smiled, too, until the words of the title of Gail's article jumped up at him from his desk.

He'd taken it upon himself to move all his belongings out of his condo into a storage unit. No use in delaying. It was time to move on. There were a garment bag and duffle bag waiting for him in the trunk of his car and Dr. Lutkin's plan had been to stay at a hotel overlooking the lake from today through the weekend. But now he had decided on other accommodations.

The basement dormitory was just as he remembered it, a sad little hole-in-the-wall, an afterthought, a last resort for weary hotel employees working odd hours, a place to take a nap and a quick shower. It was not a place to live. It held a bunk bed with two lumpy mattresses, a scratched metal desk, and a creaky swivel chair, all of which were coated with a thin layer of dust and cobwebs. After cleaning things off with rough paper towels from the shabby little adjoining bathroom, Dr. Lutkin opened his briefcase and placed Gail's article on the desk. He looked at the title again. It felt like an accusation.

WHAT AM I SO AFRAID OF?

Gail has really helped me a lot the past couple days. Yesterday as soon as my classes were over she was waiting right outside the door for me. She asked me if I was nervous about the session with my parents. And I told her I didn't want them to see me like I was, you know, with the black nail polish and everything. And Gail said we could do something about it. She got the nail polish remover from wherever the counselors keep all our contraband stuff locked up. I wasn't allowed to use it, of course, but she could. Why does it feel so cold? I like the way it feels for some reason. Anyway, while she was taking the black polish off (and using up lots of cotton balls) I told her that I was scared to talk to my parents and I told her more about what happened last Friday in the snow. It's weird that she knows about the craziest things I've ever done and was actually there when one of them happened. But maybe that makes it easier to talk to her. I told her a lot of things, even about Devante, and even about how lately I've been listening to "Can't Let Go" and "End of the Road" over & over again since they are the saddest songs in the world.

She asked me how listening to sad songs and dressing all in black and gray was making me feel. And then I realized that it only made me feel worse. What I really wanted to do was wear the clothes I like, but instead I made another uniform for myself, and I <u>HATE</u> uniforms!!! There's a part of me that wants to fit in, but another part of me that feels like I never will. I'm not like other people, so why even try to dress like them? Why not just wear something fun and surround myself with the things I find beautiful all the time, like flowers, birds, butterflies and bright colors? The past few days I've really missed that. Plus I didn't want everybody to start asking what was wrong and then end up telling my parents about how I really feel about Devante. All it would do is prove them right and then they'll be like, "Janina, you're too crazy to have a boyfriend."

It felt good to have my nails back to normal. My hands looked new. Afterwards, Gail said I should always remember that I am not my feelings. When I went to the session with my parents, Gail was right there with me, and so was Dr. Lutkin. It was nice having the 2 of them there to back me up. I needed them. I was just trying to show my parents what Matthew said about my report. He wrote "Outstanding!" on it, which would be an A at a normal school. But as usual Daddy saw it as a reason to complain about how I get to call my teachers & counselors by their first names and we don't get any grades here. He asked me if I'm doing what my teachers tell me to do, and Dr. Lutkin reminded him that I have a say in my learning process. And then my father said that I'm not going to get anywhere in life without discipline and that's why they sent me to Precious Angels, so I could learn to obey. And then I said that I can just punish myself now and I don't need anyone to do it for me. Then everyone got really quiet and Gail looked really surprised. I wasn't trying to be sarcastic or anything, just honest, just trying to speak up. We spent the rest of the time talking about what discipline means.

Today since I had a little more free time I started repainting my flowers to make them colorful again.

I still have a lot more to go. Repainting all of them will take a lot of discipline.

~~~

Pretending to be normal wears me out. I never realized how exhausting it is until this afternoon when I left this school for the first time since coming here. Now I kind of see why Janina doesn't want to leave, even though she's not scared of the same things that I am.

It's crazy that simple things like going out to eat with my brother and my friends are so hard for me to do now. At first I didn't even know where I wanted to go. Mom had taken me and Monica to so many nice restaurants over the past year. I can't even get my favorite pizza without being reminded of that time we went to Gino's East, where they let you write all over the walls, and she wrote a quote from her favorite Queen Latifah song with a permanent marker. Luckily right then I saw Marcia walking by, dressed like she just stepped out of a time machine, and I realized that we should go someplace old-fashioned like Ed Debevic's. I never went there with Monica.

I got a chance to introduce Janina to everybody

and asked her if she wanted to come with us. And like I said before, I know she's scared to leave. But I was still hoping that maybe she'd do it for me. She was just like, "Sorry, I can't," and I felt bad for asking her in front of everyone. She looked so scared and sad that I knew I needed to cheer her up. So I asked her if she wanted me to bring something back for her and she said she wanted cheese fries.

When we got there, it was so weird. Not just because it's a 50's diner and all the waiters and waitresses act like cartoon characters and dress like they came from some old TV show, but just being around so many people again, you know? Being out there was disorienting, like riding backwards on a Metra train and seeing where I'd been instead of where I was going. Not that I'm ready to turn my back on anything. I had to switch seats with Chad so I could face the doors and keep an eye on things. I never cared about stuff like that before. But now I know that anything can happen so I need to pay attention.

They all tried to talk about normal subjects like school and even asked me about what Harrison is like. I told them about the homework I have to do: going back to Whitney Park to see the lobby again. They said they want to help me with it. So we're gonna do it next Tuesday after school. Derrick said he'll stick around so he can drive me there, even though it means he will have to miss some classes. And that is a huge deal for him because he was always Mister Perfect Attendance. It's nice to know they've all got my back.

When I got back here, at first I felt good because it's all become so familiar to me now and kind of predictable. But as I climbed the stairs, it started feeling familiar in a bad way, like Valentine's Day. Here I was, headed to see a girl, bringing her a gift. I had to remind myself that this was different and nothing bad was gonna happen this time. I had to do the breathing exercises Gail taught me. I'm glad they worked for me again.

I gave Janina her fries and also the paper hat I picked up for her with the name of the restaurant on it. I guess she was pretty hungry because I have never seen that girl eat that fast before, just grubbin' with a paper hat from Ed Debevic's on her head. Then when she was done and was getting ready to throw the box away, she saw what the waitress had written on it.

I guess I forgot to mention that part. See, our waitress, who said her name was Trixie, got a little too excited when she overheard me saying that the fries were for a girl when I ordered them to go. She started asking all these questions about if we were going steady (who says that anymore?) and if I think Janina's pretty. And then she was like, "Well, Romeo, nothing says I love ya like Ed's cheese fries!" And Jerome said he thought he saw her write something on the box before she put it in the bag and brought it over to our table. Jerome was right. Trixie had written the words of an old song that was playing while we waited for our food: "Why must I be a teenager in love?"

So, yeah, Janina saw that. And she looked at me, then back at the box, then back at me again. And when she smiled at me, I didn't want to tell her anything about Trixie.

~~~

I think Devante really, really, really, really likes me!!! At least that's what the French fry box he gave me said. I was so hungry that I ate all the fries before I even read it. All I had for lunch was a salad because I knew he was coming back with cheese fries, which I haven't had in forever since Dr. Lutkin won't let us have fried food here because he says it's never too early to start watching your cholesterol. I guess that's the downside of having a doctor plan your school cafeteria menu. Naomi was watching me like a hawk because I think she thought I was gonna start starving myself like Heather & Shannon & Brittany. They have to be separated at meals because they have starving contests. Otherwise without even saying a word they'll just stare at each other's plates like they're daring each other not to eat. Crazy. No, I definitely don't want to be part of that. I like fries too much.

I wish I could have gone to lunch with Devante and his friends today. He asked me to join them, but I couldn't. No way I'm going out there. I'm still not ready. Still not normal enough. While they were out there having a good time like normal teenagers do on *Saturdays*, I had to settle for watching normal teenagers on a corny TV show, *Saved By The Bell*. The only things I like about that show are Lisa's outfits and Slater's muscles. I was in the lounge because I had followed Devante back upstairs when he went to get his coat from his room, but didn't want to look like I was following him like a crazy psycho stalker girl. So I had to play it off like I had been planning to go to the lounge all along. Then Marcia asked me to do a sketch of her and this guy Keith she likes from another old TV show she watches, *The Partridge Family*. She asked me to write "I Think I Love You" underneath the drawing since that's the title of one of his songs. I had already done one of her with Davy from *The Monkees*, another show she likes. For that one she had me write "Daydream Believer," which fits her a little too well.

I had just finished my drawing when Devante came back with a little paper hat from the restaurant that he put on my head, and the box of fries. I wish I could save the box forever, but I know that would just be hoarding, and the counselors wouldn't let me keep it. But I can't help it. I feel like my whole life is changing now. I couldn't stop smiling, and then he smiled back at me, and he has the most wonderful smile! And I don't know if it's still too soon after Monica and everything, so I don't want to ruin everything by saying something about it. And I also feel a little sad because I don't know how much longer we will get to see each other. But apparently the rumors about us having a skating party are really true. Only the party will be here in our gym, not at a rink. The counselors said something about us being too cooped up inside with all the snow and everything. And this is the closest thing we've ever had to a normal high school dance. I hope they play at least one slow song so I can skate with Devante to it. I'm gonna wear a dress with some biker shorts underneath it. And I need to figure out what to do with my hair. I want to look really fly tonight.

~~~

I can't even do something as simple as skating without buggin' out. There was a skating party in the gym last night and it started out well. I was fine until they started playing M.C. Hammer, of all things. There was this one song that Monica always made fun of, and all of a sudden it was there, in the Harrison gym. And the next thing I know, I'm in the hall outside the gym, skates off, curled up on the floor. Janina came after me and tried to help me calm down. But it didn't help. I had to go back to my room. I went to bed early. Took my sleeping pills and had more nightmares about Janina getting killed like Monica.

Today started out kinda weird because while I was down in the basement doing laundry, I could've sworn I heard one of Dr. Lutkin's records playing somewhere in the distance. I started to wonder if maybe I'm worse than I thought.

But after life skills, something cool happened. We had pet therapy. They brought cats and dogs to the lounge, really friendly ones. Everybody was really happy. Ed even took off one of his gloves to pet one of the dogs, though of course he cleaned his hand off right away with baby wipes. Alejandra's allergic to cats and dogs, but she didn't want to get left out so she took some allergy medicine. She said that all medications except the pills they give us every day make her sleepy and after a while she fell asleep in a beanbag chair with a kitten in her arms. I ended up chillin' with a golden retriever that put her head in my lap and looked up at me with the most trusting eyes. Janina said that Lucky is her favorite dog, and she must really like me. It was the calmest I felt all weekend. I wish I could be that calm all the time.

~~~

Dear Shawn,

I couldn't stay away from Harrison this weekend. I had to run the parent meeting yesterday, but I also went there again today for a little while. I got there just in time for the animal assisted therapy session where one of my patients, Ed, made a lot of progress. They say it was his first time being around the animals without wearing a surgical mask.

I have to admit that I was really there to

check on Janina. I keep wondering when Dr. Lutkin is going to read the article, or if he already has. Oddly enough I saw his car in the school parking lot, though he was not in his office. After pet therapy was over, Janina took me to her room to show me the flowers and butterflies on her wall. She had painted them black and gray because she had been prematurely grieving the loss of the boy she has started having feelings for. But this weekend she went back over the flowers with paints and has restored them to their prior brilliance. It is a definite sign of progress.

Many years ago, while still selecting the toys that he would use with his young patients in play therapy, Dr. Lutkin wandered into an antique store and found the tin knights that now kept watch over the papers on the desk. They had been so much like the ones he used to have.

"The treasures of his lonely childhood." He remembered a line he'd written in that story ages ago. It still shocked him that Dr. Thomas had somehow managed to uncover it. He had spent most of the weekend in this room, hidden away from the world. He had spent last night here at this desk, re-reading the article with the ominous title.

He asked himself why he had chosen to stay here. Simone had deposited the alumni donations into the school account. They had enough money now. He still had a salary. He still had savings. He was supposed to be looking for a new place to live, or staying in a decent hotel for a few days while he searched for one. His jazz musician friends would gladly repay his kindness by letting him stay in one of their spare rooms for a few days. But this room was the only option for lodging he considered. After placing Gail's article on the dusty little desk, he wondered: could it be that he was staying in this gloomy dungeon to punish himself?

He thought about when he first met Janina. He had started taking his patients on walks around the garden behind the school during sessions when the weather was warm. Sitting for so long every day was hard on his back. He didn't want to end up having to conduct his sessions lying on a chaise lounge, as though he were the patient of some old-fashioned Freudian psychoanalyst. She wore a simple brown school uniform, as plain as the little sparrow that hopped across the stone path in front of her and briefly brought a slight smile to her face, which for a moment was brightened like the flowers around her by the bird's cheerful manner. His memory of meeting her was now tinged more with guilt than with fondness.

He had read the article several times now, and each time he read it, his heart grew heavier. He had carried the burden of it up from his basement dwelling place and into his office. He had delayed his conversation with Dr. Thomas for far too long. Now it was Tuesday afternoon. Soon it would be time for his first weekly session with Janina. Soon it would be time for him to tell her the truth. First he wanted to speak with Dr. Thomas.

"I never took her intelligence into account when I diagnosed her," Dr. Lutkin told her, pensively stroking his beard. "It didn't seem relevant."

"But it is relevant. And could it be that the progress you think she's made lately is the result of finding another peer who's at her level? After all, Devante's very intelligent, too. I saw his test scores."

"That is a very astute observation. You were right. I made an egregious mistake. I have to tell her."

Soon Janina was in Dr. Lutkin's office. It was the first time he had ever called her away from her classes to see him. She wondered if she had done something wrong. He looked so sad.

"As your therapist, it's my job to use this treatment as a mirror that helps you to see yourself more clearly. But I'm afraid that the mirror I gave you was distorted and showed you an inaccurate picture of who you really are. Do you remember what I told you in our very first session together?"

How could Janina forget being told for the first time that she was crazy? He'd found a very gentle way to break the news to her, but still...

"Yes. You said, 'Janina, you're not like most other children. You have an illness. But if we work together, you can get well.'"

He looked like he was going to cry.

"When I told you that, I was wrong. It's true, you're not like other kids your age. But it's not because of an illness."

"Wait a minute. Are you saying that I'm...normal?" Janina approached the idea cautiously, like she was sneaking up on it from behind.

"Not just normal. *Gifted.* Your emotional sensitivity isn't the symptom of a mental illness," he explained. "It's a feature of your intelligence and creativity. There was never anything wrong with you. The intense sadness and despair you felt was all because your school and social environment didn't meet your needs. And I'm so sorry that I didn't understand that all these years."

"But you were the only one who ever really understood me!"

"No, I didn't. All these years, I *misunderstood* you. I'm sorry that I failed you."

So I just wasted four years of my life? Janina thought as she began to cry. *What do I know about normal? Sure, I recognize it in other people. But in me?*

"So what am I supposed to do now? Are you gonna kick me out and make me go back out there again?"

Where would she go? Back to her old school where the teachers might hit her again? They didn't think she was gifted. They didn't think she was anything but disobedient. Suddenly everything she thought she wanted seemed stupid.

"No. I'd never kick you out. But I think in a few weeks, you'll be ready to go. I'm putting you into the transitional program," Dr. Lutkin said.

"Really? Just like Devante?"

"Yes. It isn't too late for you to get your life back. So be brave. Go back out there. There is a place where you belong. You just need to find it."

Janina jumped up from her seat and gave Dr. Lutkin a big hug and then hurried out of his office so she could find Devante and tell him her good news.

CHAPTER 32
NOBODY LOVES A GENIUS CHILD

Dr. Lutkin stood in his doorway and watched Janina as she dashed across the lobby and up the staircase. Now that her back was turned to him, he could finally let his face show what he was truly feeling, a bottomless regret. He recalled the poem on a page he had removed from his old book of poetry before he gave it to Janina, Langston Hughes saying that "nobody loves a genius child." So sad, but seemingly true. He had been so deep in thought that he hadn't noticed that Gail had remained in the lobby and was watching him now with great concern. She got up from one of the wingback chairs and walked over to him.

"Are you all right?" she asked.

Dr. Lutkin looked at her intensely for a moment, then looked away. "My God, what have I done?"

"It was a mistake, Dr. Lutkin. We all make them."

They walked into his office and closed the door behind them. Gail took a seat in front of his desk, and Dr. Lutkin sat down behind it. She looked at the plaque on his desk again. And then she noticed the old and weather-beaten copy of *On The Road* on his bookshelf.

"Of course I've misdiagnosed patients before, but this... I was so sure about Janina's case. I never even consulted with anyone else about it because I had seen a case just like this one before."

A case just like this one? Could it be—could his brother—

"You don't have a brother, do you?"

Dr. Lutkin shook his head.

"So then the boy in the story was you? And the other case you saw, just like Janina's... it was yours?"

Dr. Lutkin took off his glasses and began to cry.

"Yes," he whispered. "I changed my name. I had to. If my family had found me, they'd have had me lobotomized. Once I got to college, I kept thinking about what I went through at that horrific institution. I decided to become a psychiatrist because I wanted to help other patients. I didn't want them to suffer as I had. I had therapy as part of my training, but I never told my therapist about my time in the hospital. There was even more of a stigma back then than there is now.

"I wish I'd done that now. I wish someone had told me my parents and doctors had been wrong. All I knew was that I once had a nervous condition, and every time I looked at Janina, I saw myself. Yet I did the same thing to her that was done to me! Carl Jung said that 'Only the wounded physician heals,' but it's hard to remain neutral when you suffer from the same issue that your patient does."

He was still reeling from what he had learned, both about Janina and about himself. He considered this his greatest professional failure. How could he have been so wrong? How could he have been so blind to who Janina was? And how had he made the mistake he'd warned Gail and so many other psychiatrists he'd trained not to make by identifying too much with a patient? For years he'd borne his devastating secret in silence, too burdened by it to share it with anyone. It was what had made falling in love with Charlotte Hoffman so hard for him. He couldn't tell her that the man she knew and loved wasn't real, that he had given himself the first name of a fictional character he'd admired when he was seventeen and had taken his last name from a concert hall he'd stopped in once while hitchhiking. He didn't want to force Charlotte to be a part of the lie he was living, and so he had devoted himself to his school instead. It was all he had. All these years it had gone so well for him, being entrusted with the most intimate details of his patients' lives while never being expected to disclose his own. He thought he'd found his ideal vocation as the keeper of other people's secrets, but now it seemed his own secret had impaired him all along.

"Four years! My God, four years!" Dr. Lutkin shook his head. Then he looked at Gail. "You should go check on her."

"But what about you?"

Only last week he had considered himself extremely fortunate. Now it seemed that his fortune had once again reversed. He had spent decades searching psychology books for traces of himself only to find that he had been chasing a phantom. He had escaped, but the cost of his liberation was steep. He was a fugitive from his own past. He had to spend his late teens constantly looking over his shoulder for fear of being found out. He grew a full beard as soon as he was able in the hope of disguising himself. He thought of all that he had missed. He had estranged himself from his family. He had chosen not to participate in any freedom rides, sit-ins, protests, or marches despite the yearning of his conscience because he didn't want to risk being arrested. He had decided to work with Dr. Olmsted because his utopian vision for mental health care gave his own idealism a safer outlet.

The year after Dr. Olmsted died, Janina came to his office for the first time. He had felt so lost then, suddenly responsible for so many things. But with her case, he felt no uncertainty, no need to consult, no reason to seek anyone else's professional opinion. If only Dr. Olmsted had been there to prevent all this. Now he needed another seasoned professional to confide in, and there was only one he could trust.

"What I need to do right now is give Dr. Hoffman a call."

CHAPTER 33
THE ONLY DIFFERENCE

The once familiar hallways seemed strange to Janina now. And she felt like a stranger to herself. How could all of this have been a mistake? A moment ago in Dr. Lutkin's office she had been so excited, but now she felt like crying. Wasn't that why they had thought she had a mood disorder, because her emotions were prone to take such sharp turns?

Why did she feel more at home here than she ever did with her parents? Her room here felt like it was her own. Her room at home seemed like a shrine to a girl who had never existed. Just who was the real Janina, anyway? And where did she really belong? Once she was back in her room she did what she'd learned to do, what had been prescribed to her as a possible treatment for her craziness: she wrote her thoughts in her journal so that she could sort them out.

This is my very own book & I'm proud to say that I'm not crazy after all. I'm still getting used to the idea. I don't know what it means. Maybe I should have stayed longer to ask Dr. Lutkin more questions. He said that he made a mistake and I was never supposed to be here. But were the last four years really a waste of time? At least I got a chance to get away from teachers who hit me, and kids who made fun of me all the time. At least at this school no one is allowed to hit you or tease you. The only paddles here are for playing ping-pong. And if you have to cry no one makes fun of you. It's the only place where I ever felt comfortable being myself.

But if it's okay to be myself, and if there's nothing really wrong with me, then maybe Dr. Lutkin & Devante are right and there really is no reason for me to be afraid to go back home again. Still, I can't help but wonder what else Dr. Lutkin was wrong about. What he told me I was is what I believed I was.

But really it started before he told me. I always knew I was different. But he was the one who told me I needed to do something about it. And I tried and I tried and I tried. But there was no point in trying. But I didn't know that then.

And what did I miss out on by being in here and not out there? Do I have to go back to Precious Angels? Do things have to go back to being how they were? I'm gonna miss the good things about being here, like getting to draw whenever I want to, and not getting screamed at by teachers all the time. What if I told my parents I'm not leaving unless I don't have to go back to Precious Angels? Then again, where would I go?

It's all so confusing. I guess I should have stayed and talked to Dr. Lutkin a little longer. My feelings are all tangled up, like the necklaces in the bottom of my jewelry box. I'm mad, I'm scared, I'm frustrated, and somehow all of those feelings are normal, and I'm normal, and I'm not my feelings. I'm just me, just Janina.

Weird, but somehow not crazy. Somehow I'm supposed to accept this about myself. Somehow, I'm supposed to learn to love myself.

Journaling wasn't as helpful this time as she hoped it would be. She thought about her graphic novel again. Writing and drawing it had always been a great escape from reality. Maybe now she could finally think of a great twist ending. What if Steffanie wasn't really depressed after all? What if her superpowers came about because she had been taking crazy pills when she wasn't even crazy? But who would believe that ending? It would seem like it just came out of nowhere unless she went back and added a few clues at the beginning. In English class, Matthew had called it foreshadowing. But Janina didn't feel like doing any foreshadowing right now.

She looked at herself in the mirror, still not sure who she really was or where she really belonged. How could the past four years have all been a mistake? But then again, at least now she could have the normal life she had been hoping for, if gifted meant normal.

Without even thinking about it, she opened the bottom dresser drawer and took Snuggle out of it. She held him close to her chest and squeezed him.

Then someone knocked on her door. She saw Gail looking through the window.

"How do you feel about what Dr. Lutkin just told you?" Gail asked when she stepped inside the room and closed the door behind her.

"I don't know." That was the most honest answer Janina could give.

"You know who else is gifted? Devante."

Janina felt a sudden warmth spreading in her chest.

"Really?"

"Yeah, and maybe that's why you two get along so well. You know he goes to a special high school for gifted kids."

Devante must have been waiting outside

because he came in right after Gail mentioned his name. Not wanting to trigger Devante, Janina hid her teddy bear behind one of her pillows.

"I'm about to visit my school right now. It's my homework. I wanted to see if you'd join me."

Janina found herself seized with sudden panic. Everything seemed to be happening too quickly.

"I don't think I'm ready." She cringed.

"You're still afraid you don't belong?"

She nodded her head.

"I'm about to do something that absolutely, positively terrifies me. Derrick and my friends are gonna be there, but it would really mean a lot to me if you came, too. And you know what? Maybe we can help each other. Maybe you can face your fears, too."

Devante was right. If she was normal, she should be able to do it. She took her coat out of her wardrobe. She had embroidered it in occupational therapy. Once she had sewn flowers and buttons all over it, she had painted parts of it, too. It had taken months, but it was her masterpiece. And then she embroidered a hat and scarf to go with it.

Gail was happy to give her permission to venture off campus with Devante. It was time.

To get to Devante's school, Derrick had to drive across the overpass that bridged the expressway. Devante stared at it silently. He was glad he hadn't jumped. He hadn't realized until just now how close his high school was to The Harrison School. Just a few blocks. Just a five minute drive.   When they pulled up in front of the building, Devante slowly got out of the car. Chad and Jerome were waiting for him. He walked up the sidewalk to the main entrance and stood in front of the doors. Janina, Derrick, Chad, and Jerome were right behind him. He took a deep breath, opened one of the doors, and walked into the lobby.

The poster of Monica was still there. Now that he was inside, though, he saw something he hadn't noticed before: all around it were notes from the other kids who knew and missed her. Kids from the track team, kids from the choir, kids from Honors Biology. They would miss her smile, her laugh, her voice, her sportsmanship. Devante was not the only one who remembered those things. He was not all alone in his grief. As he began to cry, his friends and his brother put their arms around him.

The picture of Monica made Janina feel sad. She wanted to comfort Devante, so she took his hand. And his brother and friends backed away. He stared into Monica's picture, at the unblinking eyes that would never look into his again, at the smile—the same one she had given him just minutes before her death—forever preserved in the photograph. She was gone. He would have to move on now. And he shouldn't feel guilty about it. He could move on, but still take her with him always, in his heart. He could store the memory of her like a treasure in a vault. If he could only learn to separate the good memories of her from the bad ones of what happened to her... Maybe if he kept working at it, he could.

Devante would move on slowly, gradually. Like everyone at Harrison had told him, it was a process. Holding Janina's hand in his, he was grateful to have someone else in his life who really understood what that meant. Maybe he could stop hating himself enough to let someone else in, even though he knew it meant risking another devastating loss. But maybe Janina was worth the pain.

He pulled Janina closer and embraced her. And she put her arms around him, and they were closer than they had ever been before. The two of them stood there in the lobby for a while, holding each other, not saying a word. And then they let go.

He could picture himself coming back to school again, even if it meant having to walk through these same hallways without Monica. But he still had his other friends, and Monica's friends still had their memories of her, too. Maybe there was a reason to keep living after all. He just had to keep looking.

Janina could tell something was different about Devante now. She was relieved.

"For the first time," said Devante, wiping the tears from his eyes, "I feel like I'm gonna be okay."

"I'm so glad to hear you say that," she told him.

Janina noticed a couple of kids their age were headed in her direction. One had on ripped jeans that had been put back together with safety pins. The other one had bright blue hair. Janina hoped they weren't coming to talk to her. She had no idea what to say, no idea who she even was anymore.

"Your outfit is slammin'! Where'd you get it?" the blue haired girl asked her.

"I embellished it myself," Janina said shyly. "Thanks."

"Seriously? You made that? Rock on," said the boy with the safety-pinned jeans. "We love meeting other artists. Hey, wanna check out what we're making in art club?"

But Janina didn't even go to their school! Would it be okay if she went? She turned and looked at Devante and his friends. They nodded in encouragement. So Janina followed them through the hallways of the school. It was so much bigger than Precious Angels. They finally got to the art classroom. And when she got there, she found kids wearing outfits just as wild and wonderful as what she and the blue-haired girl and the ripped-jeans boy had on. Everyone was working on art projects. There were paintings and sculptures and mosaics, and just as many art supplies as they had at The Harrison School.

"Hey everyone, this is Janina," the blue-haired girl introduced her. "She's here visiting Devante, and she's a great artist. She made her whole outfit!"

"You should make something," said a boy in an oversized flannel shirt, handing Janina some paper and some paints.

Janina felt like she was re-joining some lost tribe she had once been a part of long ago. She imagined this was what E.T. felt like when he went back home to his planet. No longer a stranger in a strange land, she had found kindred spirits. Before she knew it, she was so absorbed in what she was doing that her awkwardness faded away. And all that mattered was the painting in front of her. Her exuberance was contagious. The kids from the art club, when they took breaks from working on their own projects, came over and introduced themselves. Devante and his friends were happy to see her enjoying herself. He had never seen her smile so much. And then the art teacher spoke to her.

"You have such an incredible way with color. What school do you attend?"

Suddenly Janina was caught off guard. What was she supposed to say, that she went to a special school for crazy kids but actually she wasn't crazy?

Then Devante said, "You've probably never heard of it. It's very small, very exclusive. Almost impossible to get into."

He gave Janina a sly grin. It sounded like something his father would say, which he found both funny and a little bit frightening. She smiled back at him, relieved.

"Well if you ever decide to transfer, I'd be delighted to have you in my class," the teacher replied.

I think that's the first time any teacher ever said that about me, Janina thought.

"Thanks. I'm gonna talk to my parents about it."

It was getting late, and they needed to get back in time for dinner, and for her family session with her parents. So much had happened today. Janina would have to write about it in her journal. She thanked everyone for introducing her and letting her use their art supplies. Janina took her new artwork with her when she and Devante left. On her way out of the classroom, she noticed something on the bulletin board. There was a photo of a man with a wild, curly mustache making a funny face for the camera, a familiar face from some art books she'd read. And underneath the artist was a caption:

"The only difference between a madman and me is that I am not a madman."
—Salvador Dalí

Janina would have to ask Dr. Lutkin about it. Maybe he could explain what it meant, though she thought she might be beginning to understand it.

Devante thanked his friends for what they did for him before they headed home. Then he told Derrick he wanted to show Janina something before they got back in the car. His brother took the hint and walked ahead of them. Once his brother was gone, Devante took Janina's hand. The tingling she felt in it when he touched her spread all the way to her toes. She felt so bright, so happy, so alive inside. Palms pressed together, fingers intertwined, they continued walking hand in hand through the hallways and back outside.

"Are you sure you're going to be okay?" Devante's mother asked.

Devante smiled and told her he'd be fine. He straightened his tie, made of orange, red, and blue kente cloth from Ghana. From backstage he and his mother could hear the buzz of the audience as they took their seats in the community center's auditorium. A lot of people were coming to the talent show today, more than they had expected. He was excited about playing his new music, especially since he wanted to see the look on his father's face when he heard what he had done with Chopin and Rachmaninoff. He knew his dad loved classical and hated hip-hop. He, Chad, and Jerome had decided to take their interest in music more seriously after Devante got home from the Harrison School. Doing music therapy and listening to old records with Dr. Lutkin had helped him see how important music was in his life, and made him realize how much he wanted to write his own songs instead of just mastering the works of famous composers. The song they would be performing today was special because it was dedicated to Monica, who had died two years ago this month. This would also be the very first public event at the community center his mom had named in Monica's honor, which was opening just in time for Black History Month.

He was glad they had such a good turnout. He peeked his head out from behind the stage curtains and saw a lot of familiar faces in the audience. Even Ed had made it. He was going to a boarding school now, a high school out in the western suburbs where he took a lot of math and science classes. Maybe they could have another free throw contest in the community center's gym later.

Gail smiled when she saw Devante. She was glad he was doing so well now. He had really turned a corner the day he went back to visit his high school with Janina, his brother, and his friends, though his recovery was not without setbacks. He'd still had to sort out his feelings about what had happened to Monica and reconcile them with his new feelings for Janina. But she helped him resolve them. When his nightmares and flashbacks subsided, he was finally ready to return home.

His last day there, at the end of June, was also Gail's last day. She had to move on so that she could begin her new residency. The time had flown by. She would be finished in a few months. Fortunately, she had already found a position. Starting in August, she would be working with Dr. Lutkin at the Harrison School again, though this time she would be the assistant director. She hoped that she would also have time to volunteer her services to the new community center.

She was so happy for Devante's mother. It had taken her a long time to secure permits and renovate this old building, but the results were stunning. It reminded her of The Harrison School with its joyful use of color. And she would recognize the mural in the front lobby anywhere. She knew Janina's style when she saw it.

"Did you see this program?" Her date nudged her.

This was their third time going out, and she really liked him.

"No, let me see."

She took the program from him. And she knew the artwork on the front, which depicted the faces of such notable African-Americans in the arts as Duke Ellington, Ella Fitzgerald, Paul Robeson, and Maya Angelou, was Janina's work, too.

"Young Gifted and Black," Gail read the elaborate, hand-lettered title aloud. "Yes, I know the artist."

Across the room from Gail, Dr. Lutkin watched as Devante strode confidently onto the stage and took a seat at the piano. He thought about the condition Devante was in the first time they'd met, broken, undernourished, sleep-deprived, and unwilling to speak. To see him now and realize that he had a part in this young man's transformation was an honor, and so was being invited to witness this performance. Moments like this were what made his work worthwhile.

During Devante's last few sessions at The Harrison School, the two of them had often talked about music. Dr. Lutkin had introduced Devante to jazz; Devante had introduced Dr. Lutkin to hip-hop. Dr. Lutkin had seen music as an emotional anchor in Devante's life and encouraged him to try writing his own songs. When Devante called to invite him to hear his new song, Dr. Lutkin knew he had to come. He had often been wary of accepting such invitations, not always certain he would feel welcomed, concerned that his presence would be an unpleasant reminder of a former patient's difficult past. Of course, the recent flood of letters he had received from so many of them had made him reconsider his reluctance.

Still, when he saw Janina this afternoon talking with a group of girls her age in the lobby before the talent show began, he decided not to go over and speak to her. He didn't want to put her in the awkward position of having to introduce him to her friends. But maybe after the program was over he could say hello. His wife, Dr. Charlotte Hoffman-Lutkin, had seen Janina's patchwork-embellished wool peacoat and wanted to compliment her on it.

Dr. Hoffman-Lutkin knew all about what had

happened with Janina. In fact, she had even interviewed her for her new book about the misdiagnosis of gifted children. Janina's case was what had brought the couple back together. Dr. Lutkin had needed someone to confide in, and he told her everything. The more time they spent together, the more they both realized what had been missing from their lives all this time. In all the years that they had been apart, their feelings for each other hadn't changed. Dr. Lutkin was glad to have found someone he could trust with his secret.

Whenever he thought about the convoluted path his life had taken, Dr. Lutkin felt overwhelmed. After he had run away when he was seventeen, he had been determined to go through life as though his frailties did not exist. But he had never expected that he would end up making the same errors that his own doctors had made over forty years earlier. He had never thought that the labels he had been given would still define and shame him, never realized that he could be such a stranger to himself, even after so many years of careful introspection. How horrifying it had been to repeat the worst of his own history with Janina. The entire realization had been a bitter pill to swallow.

Dr. Hoffman-Lutkin had been the one to convince him not to stop working with Janina despite the terrible guilt he felt for having misdiagnosed her. And it was good that she did, because finding out that nothing was wrong with her made Janina feel even more unsure of herself than believing that she was crazy ever had.

Janina's last few weeks living at the school hadn't been easy. She started having trouble sleeping. She stopped drawing and started making collages cut from magazines and quilts from scraps of fabric because she felt like she needed to piece her identity back together. And if that wasn't hard enough, her parents' reaction made things even more complicated.

Instead of being angry at Dr. Lutkin for his mistake, her parents saw it as a miracle. Instead of realizing that there had never been anything wrong with her, they thought she had finally been healed. But the good thing was they began to listen to her more.

As Gail and Dr. Lutkin helped Janina to figure out what she wanted and who she really was, she felt more comfortable telling her mother and father that she wanted to go to high school with Devante, and not back to Precious Angels. Gail and Dr. Lutkin helped to convince her parents that Janina needed to go to school with other gifted students. But she didn't want to start at a new school so close to the end of the school year. It made no sense to her. Working together, they found a solution. Janina went home to live with her parents, but her father dropped her off at The Harrison School for classes every day. She had the same teachers, but unlike the other kids, she had homework. She needed to get used to doing it again so that she would be ready to go to Whitney Park in the fall. She had already passed the test to get into the school, but her teachers wanted to be sure she would be able to keep up with the workload. When she came back home, her parents let her redecorate her bedroom so that it was more like the room she had at Harrison, full of the flowers and butterflies and art that she made.

From April until June, she and Devante had opposite schedules, with her living at home and taking classes at Harrison, and him living at Harrison but taking classes at Whitney Park. They saw each other briefly each weekday, after Tom dropped him off and before her father picked her up, and were finally reunited during their Saturday transitional students group meeting. They also ended up in Whitney Park's summer school together, and finally, back in regular classes in the fall.

Her social circle slowly widened as Devante introduced her to his friends and as she met other young artists in her new school's art club and at the weekend classes at the Art Institute that her new art teacher encouraged her to take. Soon, between all her extracurriculars, her new friends, and the tons of homework that Devante had warned her about, she was so busy on weekends that she didn't have time to help out at her mother's hair salon or go to the Friday night youth services at church. On the rare occasions that she did see the mean kids who used to tease her, they treated her with the same kind of aloof respect that the other church members had for those they believed had been touched by divine intervention. They wouldn't dare torment Janina now. Instead, they kept their distance.

Some days, she still couldn't believe how different her life was now. Today was like that. Just two years ago she was starting to believe that she would never be normal, and now she had friends and people who liked her artwork. Her only friends two years ago had been a girl who thought she was a TV character and a boy who wouldn't talk. Now Kelly (formerly Marcia) was going by her real name, living with a good foster family, and shopping at Old Navy instead of thrift stores. And Janina and Devante had so much to say to each other that they tied up their parents' phone lines calling each other and exchanging messages online. And this afternoon, Devante was about to play a song that had taken him two years to write.

These were the kinds of things she still wrote down in her journal. She had a new one with her, open on her lap. She liked it because it had alternating lined and unlined pages so she could write and draw in the same place. As she watched Devante start playing his new song, she felt her hand wander down the page, sketching the contours of his face. He didn't like to pose for her, so she always had to catch him when he was busy doing something else. She had done her best drawings of him when he was playing the piano. Maybe she would write a new graphic novel and he could be one of the characters. Or maybe she'd design an album cover for him someday. But for now, she would listen as he played, hearing all the feelings he could only communicate with his notes and chords.

Everything was pouring out of Devante now, his sadness over Monica's loss, his anger about the senseless violence that had taken her young life, the despair and anguish he once felt, his relief when he saw her killers brought to justice, his new hope for his own life now that he'd recovered. And Jerome's rap lyrics and the jazz samples that Chad scratched in on the turntables only enhanced it. The song was more than just music to all of them. It was a memorial. When it ended everyone in the audience rose to their feet with applause and several people had to wipe the tears from their eyes, including Devante.

When the talent show was over and everyone exited to the lobby, Janina's painting of Monica smiled down on them from a mural. She had been inspired to create something like what she had seen in the hallways of The Harrison School. Whether she was supposed to have been there or not, the school had become a part of her, and she took it with her everywhere she went. And when she took Devante's hand and walked with him across the crowded lobby so they could talk to Gail and Dr. Lutkin, she felt grateful to have found a place where she had been listened to and understood for the first time in her life. She was grateful, too, that she was still finding new places that felt like home. She and Devante hoped that Monica's Place would be like that for everyone in the neighborhood.

AUTHOR'S NOTE

First, please note that I have put this note at the end of the book for a reason, as there are numerous spoilers ahead. Next, some things that should be pretty obvious: *A Bitter Pill to Swallow* is a work of fiction and I am not a mental health professional. Though I did a great deal of research, I deliberately limited myself to books that were published before and during the time period in which the story is set. So some of the story's contents are outdated. New discoveries have been made since the 90s, and I am certainly not an expert. In fact, when I was on *Jeopardy!* the final question was about a new blood test that detects depression, and I got it wrong because at that time I had been so focused on my research that the headline I'd read about the new test barely registered with me.

New and more effective drugs are being developed all the time that can treat mental illnesses. There are also numerous alternative therapies, but that's outside the scope of this book. If you have been prescribed medications to treat a mental illness and would prefer a different form of treatment, you should talk to a professional about it before changing anything.

Yes, it is possible for someone to be both gifted and mentally ill. It's known as being "twice exceptional." However, from the beginning, I was interested in creating a character who was misunderstood, misdiagnosed, and mistakenly believed that something was wrong with her, which is why I decided not to make Janina twice exceptional.

The moral of this little story is this: don't stop taking your meds just because of Dr. Lutkin.

DISCUSSION QUESTIONS

Each of the characters could be said to have "a bitter pill to swallow." What difficult truths did they have a hard time accepting?

In what ways are the four main characters similar to each other? In what ways are they different?

If the story had been set in the present day, what would be different about it? What would still be the same?

ACKNOWLEDGEMENTS

First, I'd like to thank God for the inspiration to write this story. Next, I must acknowledge the debt of gratitude I owe to Dr. Stephen Luce, who let me visit the Orthogenic School for my research. I'd like to thank the writing instructors I've had who took the time to encourage me over the years, particularly Ms. Mollison, Mr. Littwin, Jackie White, Jacqueline Stewart, and Claudia Allen. I have a special acknowledgement for Maureen McLane, who introduced me to the beat generation in my first humanities class at University of Chicago. Thank you to all the art teachers who taught me the skills I used to illustrate my covers, especially Ryan Kapp, Andy Conklin, and Javier Chavira. I want to thank Mare Swallow for getting me involved with the Chicago Writers Conference. I'm grateful to my editors, Shanda Siler and Rebecca Heyman, and to Kalisha Buckhanon and Cal Armistead for the beautiful blurbs. A special thank you is due to Lonnie Edwards, who I am very much looking forward to working with, hopefully in the near future. I appreciate the feedback I got from my readers: Darrell Gholar, Wendell Etherly, Adewole Abioye, Niyati Mavinkurve, Katelyn Oates, Daryl Hudson, Christian Smooth, and Dr. Katie McBrine. Thanks to Dr. Alisha Thomas for helping me with my research by telling me about what it was like to go to medical school, and to Dr. Douglas Eby for his help regarding the misdiagnosis of gifted children. Shout-out to Cameron Rayburn and Intaba Shauri for refreshing my memories of early 90's hip-hop and introducing me to songs I missed out on. I'd be wrong if I didn't give credit to my brother, John Christopher Gholar, who coined the phrase "toy cops." Thanks to all my friends and family who have supported me on this journey. Finally, I'd like to thank Nancy, Rhonda, Jaclyn, Sasha, Shana, and Jeff for helping me to stay sane. This book would not have been possible without you.

OTHER BOOKS BY TIFFANY GHOLAR

Post-Consumerism

A year after graduating and not being able to find a good job with my degree, I decided to go back to school to study what I had always wanted to learn: painting. As I repurposed discarded materials for my paintings, I discovered the artistic purpose of my life. This book tells the story of my circuitous journey to creating my first major body of work as an artist. More than just an exhibition catalogue, this book highlights the events in my life that inspired my work while featuring large color photos of finished paintings and works in progress. This is the story of Post-Consumerism. This is a story of reinvention.

Imperfect Things

In 2010, I got my own art studio. I finally had a space dedicated to making artwork. But was following my dreams worth the risk? Would I ever find the right audience for my work? Could I stay motivated to keep painting despite all the times I returned from shows with unsold artwork and an empty wallet? With everything else falling apart, how would my artistic vision come together? This is the story of three years in my life when everything changed.

The Doll Project

Is Barbie to blame for giving girls body image issues, or are there larger forces at work? The Doll Project explores the influence of visual culture and societal norms while caricaturing and satirizing unattainable standards of beauty. In a world where girls gather online to remind each other that "nothing tastes as good as thin feels" and diet ads ask "what will you gain when you lose," even Barbie is never thin enough. The Doll Project dramatizes this quest for perfection in miniature. Each picture tells a story from my perspective as an ambivalent doll collector who has a love/hate relationship with the fashion industry. The photographs in this series show how both the iconic fashion doll and the fashion world around her have changed in the decades since her introduction, and culminate in a dynamic poster designed to remind women and girls to love and accept themselves no matter what they look like.

All books are available in hardcover, paperback, and ebook formats from Amazon, the iTunes Store, and Etsy.

CPSIA information can be obtained
at www.ICGtesting.com
Printed in the USA
LVHW041136041118
595902LV00001B/11/P

9 781364 467142